MYSTERY OF THE
UNINVITED GUEST

Your TRIXIE BELDEN Library

Trixie Belden and the
MYSTERY OF THE
UNINVITED GUEST

BY KATHRYN KENNY

Cover by Jack Wacker

GOLDEN PRESS
Western Publishing Company, Inc.
Racine, Wisconsin

CONTENTS

MYSTERY OF THE
UNINVITED GUEST

The Suitcase Mix-Up • 1

NEITHER OF HER TEEN-AGE BROTHERS saw the flash of light at the end of the lane, but Trixie Belden did. She suddenly wailed, "She's here! She's in my room, and she's doing it again. She's spying on me!"

"Huh?"

"Who?"

The boys' muttered questions blended with the grumbling motor of Brian's old car. Brian steered a careful course around the scooter Bobby had left near a lilac bush at the edge of the road. He flicked an anxious glance toward Trixie, who sat beside him. In the backseat, Mart struck a wooden Indian pose. He propped his chin on Trixie's shoulder. Shading his

13

eyes, he lowered his voice to its rock-bottom level. "If Belden maiden in distress show light to heap brave brothers—"

"Aw, cut it out, Mart," Brian said good-naturedly. "Can't you see that Trix is about to blow her stack? And since Moms has been with Bobby all day, she needs peace and quiet, not another fight to referee."

"Who's fighting?" Mart asked with a teasing grin, and his face could easily have been a reflection of Trixie's, so alike were they in coloring, features, and bone structure.

"*I* am!" Trixie snapped. In frustration, she pounded her knees with both fists, causing her short sandy curls to bounce against Mart's nose. His loud sneeze wasn't make-believe. "Now you're covering me with germs!" she yelled. "What chance do I have?"

"I know," Brian interrupted in his best doctor-to-be manner. "You're spied upon, teased, and completely unappreciated. But whom are you accusing of spying? Moms?"

"Moms!" Trixie's round blue eyes widened with shock. "I didn't say that. I didn't even suggest it! Why—why—Moms wouldn't—I mean she couldn't—"

"Then who?" Brian asked. He stopped the car in a graveled drive that led to the door of a comfortable farmhouse—the house in which Beldens had lived for three generations. The lawns, flower and vegetable gardens, orchards, and fields of Crabapple Farm dozed in the summer sun. Reddy, the Irish setter, had raised his head from a nest of cool grass at the sound of the car. He woofed sleepily, subdued proof that Bobby, an energetic first grader, was not outside. Trixie herself was the only discordant element in the whole pleasant scene.

Before answering Brian's question, Trixie craned her neck to peer at the second-story windows of her room. Her eyes darkened as she pressed her lips in an angry line. "She's up there," Trixie declared. "I saw the curtains move!" With her best friend, Honey Wheeler, Trixie planned to become a detective and had already solved a number of baffling mysteries. When a curtain moved, she saw it. And when light reflected off a pair of binoculars pushed between those same curtains, she saw that, too.

"Hallie Belden! That's who!" Trixie declared, finally answering Brian.

"Hallie?" both boys asked in one voice.

Mart jumped out onto the gravel. The greeting forming on his lips was never given because Trixie delivered a sharp kick to his ankle that sent him hopping toward the back porch. "Must you resort to violence?" he asked plaintively as he rubbed his ankle. "I was only—"

"I know what you were only," Trixie retorted. "Before we do all the meeting and greeting that's expected of us, we've got to have a plan of action. Trouble on two feet—that's Hallie Belden!"

"Since when?" Brian asked. Pocketing his ignition key, he walked past Trixie for a quick look at Mart's ankle. "You'll live" was his professional opinion. Then he faced Trixie, waiting to hear an explanation of her accusation.

Trixie gulped down a lump of misery. All the memories she had ever registered of her cousin from Idaho tumbled through her head like marbles in a tin can. Mr. Belden and his brother insisted that their daughters were too much alike to ever be friends. But Trixie was equally sure they were "not one smidgen alike!"

If Trixie couldn't sort out her own feelings about Hallie, how could she explain them to her brothers? She hadn't even told them Hallie was coming, though she'd known it since the afternoon a week ago when she'd overheard her mother talking long-distance with Hallie's mother.

Dangerously close to tears, Trixie said stiffly, "Let's go meet her." There was some resentment in her voice. After all, Brian and Mart weren't just her brothers; they were fellow members of a very select club, the Bob-Whites of the Glen. They should accept her judgment without question. So there!

At that moment the back door opened, and Mrs. Belden stepped onto the porch. She was followed by a tall, lean, sunbrowned girl with eyes the color of ripe blackberries. The nails of her bare feet were painted green, and her black hair was long and smooth. She wore cutoff jeans and a tank top.

"Children," Mrs. Belden said brightly, "we have company!"

"Remember me?" the girl drawled. "I'm Hallie."

Both Brian and Mart hurried up the steps, hands outstretched. Trixie lagged behind. This summer of her fourteenth year had been going so well. What had she done to deserve a visit from a cousin who'd outgrown her by three inches? Merely by looking through a veil of long black lashes, Hallie reduced two teen-age boys to pulp. If she did this to Brian and Mart, who were her cousins and therefore somewhat immune, what would she do to Dan Mangan—and—

The thought was so prickly that Trixie tried not to finish the sentence, but her stubbornly logical mind whispered, *and to Jim Frayne!*

In the commotion of "How are you?" "Wow! Look at you, all grown-up!" and "Did you have a good trip?" no one noticed that Trixie hadn't climbed the steps. Reddy sensed her mood and rose from his comfortable spot on the grass. He pushed his nose into her palm and wiggled his head to fit her scratching fingers to his itches.

Hallie made the first move. She stepped past her grinning male cousins to speak directly to Trixie. "Hi, Trix. So, you're a detective now!"

Trixie stammered, "H-How—"

"I've been catching Hallie up on news," Mrs. Belden said.

Trixie climbed the wooden steps and stood on tiptoe, prepared to kiss Hallie's brown cheek if it killed her.

Hallie sidestepped and stuck out a tanned hand for

shaking. "No kissy-kissy stuff," she said crisply.

"Fine," Trixie said, just as crisply. "No kissy-kissy." Knowing that the others were watching and listening, she felt her ears burning.

"Dad is going to Switzerland to a mining conference," Hallie announced. "Mom wanted to tag along, so I just said, 'Blessings, kids. I'll give Trix a hand at whatever she's up to.'" Hallie slid a sidelong glance at Brian and Mart and grinned. "I hope it's fun."

Trixie was glad Hallie's grin didn't include dimples. Her mouth was wide and thin-lipped. With relief at having found a flaw, Trixie began to relax. Then an imp inside her head whispered, *Does everybody like dimples, or do you think so just because you have them?*

"Honey Wheeler and I just finished a case," Trixie told Hallie.

"They managed to get all of us Bob-Whites involved," Mart put in.

"Don't they always?" Brian teased.

"Bob-Whites," Hallie repeated. She rolled her eyes and said, "Now I've heard everything. I'm a cousin to bird-watchers."

Trixie floundered for an answer. Practicing to become a full-fledged detective and sharing the chairmanship of the Bob-Whites with Jim Frayne were the two most important interests in her whole life. When her father said, "Write to Hallie," Trixie wrote. Certainly she'd written about the club, of service given to the needy, and of mysteries solved. Didn't Hallie Belden read her own mail? And quite often the Bob-Whites had been written up in newspapers outside the Hudson River valley. Hallie must read newspapers in that mining town in Idaho!

Brian knew Trixie had been edgy for days. Her well-known hair-trigger temper was set to go off, so he decided to respond to Hallie. "You haven't been here for a couple of years, so maybe you don't know about our little club."

"Little!" Trixie flared.

Brian ignored her and riveted his attention on Hallie. Mart, too, turned to Hallie. "Some of us live too far from Sleepyside to take part in after-school activities, so we've organized our own club," Brian explained. "We fixed up the old gatehouse on the Wheeler property for a clubhouse, and we even have our own station wagon, donated by Mr. Wheeler."

"Well, lah-di-dah!" Hallie drawled.

Trixie flushed. "We work!" she loudly defended their club. "We work hard, and we earn the money to pay our dues. Even Jim works—and he's inherited piles of money—and Honey works—and her family owns half this valley. What they don't own, Di's folks do—"

"Hey," Mart said, "don't leave out the Beldens. We own some of this county, too, you know!"

Trixie whirled fiercely on him. "You're making us sound like a bunch of snobs, and we're not! Honey Wheeler has a houseful of servants, but she peels

19

potatoes better than I do, and so does Di Lynch!"

"Even Bobby can do that," Mart retorted.

"Children, children!" Mrs. Belden waved her hands to fan away some of the steam from the heated encounter. Behind her the screen door slammed, and Bobby, the youngest Belden, came out of the house, pretending to yawn. Shrewdly his mother studied his performance. "Bobby," she chided, "you didn't take a nap. What have you been up to?"

"Well. . . ." Bobby widened his blue eyes to include the whole group in an innocent stare. "There was this suitcase, and it wasn't locked."

"Trixie," Mrs. Belden ordered, "go see what's happened to Hallie's belongings."

"Nothing happened to 'em," Bobby said. "They're in the middle of my bed, and they smell funny."

"Something must have spilled," Hallie declared.

Trixie ran, but Hallie ran faster. She overtook Trixie on the stairs and was the first to reach the second-floor hall. Trixie jerked open her own bedroom door, but Hallie went to Bobby's room.

"You're lost!" Trixie shouted, then stared at the unbleached muslin spread that covered her bed. It was as smooth as she had left it that morning. No suitcase, no spilled cologne.

Bobby's bedroom was across the hall, and Trixie ran to the door. Her mother was right. Bobby's bedspread wasn't even wrinkled, so he hadn't napped. And, there was a suitcase!

"Why'd you go to your room?" Hallie asked.

"I—" Trixie paused. It was a little awkward, letting Hallie suspect that she'd expected to find the suitcase in her own room because she'd seen binoculars behind a curtain there.

Hallie waved a long, slim hand at Bobby's bed. The middle of it was heaped with a jumble of a boy's camping clothes. Right on top of the heap was a pair of washable sneakers, at least size eleven. Both of Hallie's narrow bare feet could be squeezed into one of those shoes. Bobby was right—those shoes smelled.

"It isn't my bag," Hallie said.

"I can see that." Trixie walked toward the bed. "Whose is it?"

"How would I know? It's your house, and you're the detective!"

Trixie studied her cousin's thin brown face suspiciously. Was this some kind of trick? If so, it wouldn't be the first time Hallie had made trouble for her. In the past, Trixie had been the one to end up in the family doghouse because she lost her temper while Hallie remained calm. *This time*, Trixie decided firmly, *I won't bite. If Hallie's playing a trick, it's on her.*

Trixie snapped her fingers. "Well, where's your suitcase? I'll help you put your clothes away."

"I just told you," Hallie said slowly and distinctly. "This isn't my bag."

"You mean, you've already hung up your clothes, and—" While speaking, Trixie crossed the room and flung open Bobby's closet door. Nothing that would belong to Hallie could be seen.

Hallie crossed her arms. "Well?" she drawled.

"Your clothes are in my closet!" Trixie dashed from Bobby's room into her own room. Again she flung open the closet door, certain that Hallie was playing one of the tricks she'd played when they were children. She shouted, "There!"

Again Trixie stared. Her own clothes, uncrowded and unmoved from their usual positions, hung from the long clothes bar. When Trixie turned her blond head, she saw that Hallie was leaning against the doorjamb, watching quietly.

"Well, sweet cousin?" Hallie gibed.

Furiously Trixie shouted, "I know there's some kind of trick. There always is! Now, Hallie Belden, you'd just better tell me what's going on!"

"No, my dear daughter, you'd better tell *me* what's going on."

"Dad!" Trixie gasped. "How long have you been standing there?"

"Long enough to decide that you owe an apology to our guest," Mr. Belden said firmly. "I thought two years of separation might have eased old strains, but I see I was wrong." He put an arm around his tall young niece's shoulders and kissed her forehead. "How are you, Hallie? It's good to see you. Did you have a pleasant trip?"

"I'm glad to see you, too, Uncle Peter."

Mr. Belden turned to Trixie. He wore a baffled expression. "Trixie—" he began hesitantly.

"I know, Dad," Trixie said. "I've done it again. I've lost my temper before Hallie and I have been together ten minutes." Stiffly she said to her cousin, "I'm sorry. I thought—"

"It's okay, Trix," Hallie said. "You thought my longer legs were the only thing about me that's changed. You may not believe this, Trix—" Hallie suddenly looked embarrassed. She rubbed the polished hardwood floor with a bare toe. After a long silence she said abruptly, "Aw, skip it." Her wide mouth stretched in its dimpleless grin. "Since you had no mystery to solve, I've delivered one. Let's have a look at that suitcase."

What Did Bobby See? • 2

Mr. BELDEN LEFT the room after giving an approving pat to each girl's shoulder. Although he had said nothing more about the scene in Trixie's room, words were not necessary. Trixie knew how he felt about his family and his home. Beldens at Crabapple Farm had put all their love and skill into building and preserving a gracious setting. The very rugs they walked on had been hooked in bright wools by Peter Belden's grandmother. *One Belden isn't being very gracious,* whispered Trixie's conscience.

As she followed Hallie to Bobby's room, Trixie's lashes dampened with tears she dared not shed. She liked people. Usually she got along well with everyone. Certainly she always made a special effort to make a guest feel at home. That was part of being a Belden.

Family was important to her, and Hallie was family. A cousin only one year younger, a guest back in the house after a long absence, should make for one of the happiest months of the year. But—childhood's rivalry remained. The minute Hallie showed up, Trixie's bones became butter to be melted down by some kind of heat she produced within herself.

Mr. Belden was a banker in Sleepyside, and Trixie had inherited his analytical mind. This had helped her to solve numerous mysteries. She had a sixth sense that warned her of the presence of a mystery. Now she sensed that no matter what adventure grew from the suitcase mix-up, Trixie Belden faced the biggest mystery of all, the mystery of self—the enormously important question, Who am I?

Finding an answer must include knowing Hallie. Mentally Trixie had convicted Hallie of spying with binoculars and of lying about the suitcase, even though the law held one to be innocent until proved guilty. Trixie knew she had hastily jumped to a conclusion before the facts were in.

"That's no way to solve a mystery," she muttered.

"What did you say, Trix?"

Trixie flushed. "Don't mind me, Hallie. I'm always talking to myself."

"Me, too," Hallie confessed. "It helps me to think. Sometimes my ears have more sense than my eyes."

Soberly the cousins looked at each other. *Maybe,* Trixie thought, *Dad's right. Maybe Hallie and I are a little bit alike. We both like mysteries, and we both talk to ourselves. That's a beginning.*

Side by side, Trixie and Hallie stared down at the jumble of boy's clothing heaped in the middle of Bobby's bed. Trixie asked, "Who put the suitcase here?"

"I carried it from the taxi and put it on the bed myself," Hallie said.

"Didn't you notice—" Trixie began, then closed her mouth. Of course Hallie hadn't noticed that the bag wasn't hers. And that meant the wrong bag was the same size and color as Hallie's own suitcase. "It's obviously a case of a mix-up at the depot."

"Airport," Hallie corrected. "I flew."

There I go again, jumping to conclusions, Trixie thought. Aloud, she asked, "Didn't you have to present your baggage ticket?"

Hallie arched her brows. "Sure, but there was a scramble. I dropped my ticket just as my bag showed up on the baggage turntable. I was afraid that it would whirl right past me and I'd have to wait for it to come around again, so I grabbed the bag, then looked for my ticket. A man said, 'I saw this claim stub fall. Is it yours?' I didn't have time to check and just took it. The man turned and walked away, and so did I."

"Hey, what's holding up the parade?" Mart called. Feet thumped up the stairs, and both Mart and

26

Brian skidded to a stop in front of the open door.

Hallie drawled, "Come on in. I'm decent."

"We've been hearing about the baggage mix-up," Brian said. He looked straight at Trixie.

"So, my voice carries!" Trixie snapped, then flushed and avoided Brian's eyes. She prodded among some rolled-up socks on the bed. "Do you suppose the binoculars are in this mess?" she asked.

"Binoculars!" If they'd practiced registering surprise in unison, Brian, Mart, and Hallie couldn't have done a better job.

"Where did you get that idea?" Hallie asked.

"Uh, this is camping stuff," Trixie mumbled. "I thought that somewhere in this pile there should probably be a pair of binoculars."

Mart made a messy but thorough examination of the contents of the suitcase. "Wrong," he said. "No binoculars."

From his tone, Trixie knew he was remembering her outburst in the lane. She was not the only Belden with brains. Mart pretended to be a clown and liked to use outlandishly long words and sentences, but he was an honor roll student. He had good recall.

"Since I won't be dressing for dinner, will someone help me repack this bag, please?" Hallie invited.

"Speaking of dressing," Trixie said, "did you wear that outfit on the plane, Hallie?"

Hallie was no giggler. She chuckled and retorted slangily, "Nope. I tried to get away with it, but Mom sent me back to change after my bag was locked. I shoved my cutoffs and topper into my overnight kit so I could change the minute I got here." She shrugged. "Lucky I did, or else I'd be teetering around in high heels, nylons, and a double-knit suit."

Almost against her will, Trixie chalked up another point they had in common. "I like comfortable clothes, too," she said. She dropped a pair of red socks and bent to pick them up.

There on the floor, just at the edge of the hem of Bobby's bedspread, was a black plastic lid of some sort. When she turned it over on her palm, she discovered the word "Empire" printed in silver on the black surface. She held out her hand to show her find. "What do you suppose this is?" she asked.

"Looks like a lens guard from a pair of binoculars," Brian said.

"I told you—" Trixie began hotly, then forced herself to calm down. After all, Hallie had seemed honestly surprised at the mention of binoculars. And Moms said that she'd been telling Hallie all the news. That meant that Hallie couldn't have been alone in Trixie's room, spying down the lane. Then, who . . . ?

"Bobby!" Trixie shouted. "Come here!"

Instantly Bobby came through the door, wearing his angel face. Plaintively he said, "You don't have to yell at me. I've been up here a long time. This is my room, and you didn't even say 'Come in.'"

Trixie snatched the lens guard from Brian's hand and waggled it before Bobby's face. "Have you seen this before?" she demanded sternly.

Bobby took the cap and shoved it into a pocket.

"Oh, no, you don't!" Trixie warned. She reached into his pocket and came up with two lens caps. She said severely, "Now! I want to know where you put the binoculars!"

Bobby looked worried and turned to Brian for support. Trixie and Mart, the almost-twins, often gave him trouble, but Brian could be depended on to listen to his side of a story. Bobby told this tall, dark, quiet brother, "I didn't steal the—the—"

"Binoculars?" Brian prompted.

Bobby nodded. "I just wanted to borrow the nocklers to see if anybody was sitting in the wheelchair."

Around the room, lips formed the word "wheelchair," but no one made a sound. Brian held up a warning hand to keep Trixie from speaking. "Well?" he asked. "Did you see?"

"Course not. You drove in front, and I couldn't."

Mart grinned broadly. "Bobby, are you telling us that there was a wheelchair in our lane and our female shamus didn't see it?"

Bobby refused to commit himself. "What's a shame-us?"

"Mart's trying to be funny," Trixie said impatiently. "It's a policeman."

"Oh." Bobby thought deeply. "I think we need one, 'cause it's against the law."

The Beldens were used to Bobby's way of talking in circles. He could not be hurried.

"What's against the law?" Trixie asked.

"Opening other people's mailboxes." Bobby turned around and started to leave the room.

"You come right back here, Bobby Belden!" Trixie commanded.

Bobby was not to be easily ordered around just because there was a guest in the house. He was his own man. "Well, don't you want the nocklers? I was just going to get them. They're under your bed." And out the door he went.

Trixie started to follow, but Brian shook his head. With furious speed she began repacking the brown suitcase. At the bottom of the jumble she found a boy's bathing suit—knitted, knee-length, black and white trunks. The wearer would look like an escaped convict.

Hallie saw them and reddened. "May I use the telephone?"

Barely able to control her curiosity, Trixie told her, "The extension is in the hall by the dormer window seat. The phone book has a cretonne cover."

"I know my own number." Hallie's flat brown cheeks glowed with embarrassment. "I think I've solved the mystery of the bag mix-up. I'll let you know for sure after I've talked to Mom. I promised to call her anyway."

Hallie's call to Idaho was brief. She came back to Bobby's room to find her older Belden cousins sitting on the bed, waiting for her.

"My bag will be delivered at the airport," she announced. "There were two bags in our hall—the one Cap brought back from camp and the one I borrowed from Knut because it held more junk than mine. I grabbed the wrong one."

Trixie felt like a balloon slowly losing its air. She had been all set to call the airport. Now there was no reason for her to get involved. There was no mystery.

"I feel like an idiot," Hallie confessed. "When I remembered dropping my ticket, I suspected the worst. I didn't even really look at Cap's grubbies. I do that sometimes—I overlook the obvious."

"Me, too," Trixie said weakly.

Bobby appeared at the door with the binoculars and a message. "Moms says Trixie will please come set the table, and Mart and Brian can shuck the corn 'cause it's time to cook it." He waited for Brian to reach the door, then walked tall with the weight of Brian's arm on his shoulders. "I'll pull off the corn hair you miss," he promised Brian. That was Bobby's thank-you for not getting a scolding.

At Crabapple Farm, the kitchen was the center of the household. The large room was bright with polished maple, braided rugs, and gleaming copper. Treasured china waited on plate racks and cup hooks. All the kitchen niches smelled of good food and held echoes of cheerful voices.

Mr. Belden came to the porch with two dozen ears of the first garden corn. Brian, Mart, and Bobby met him with a dishpan. Trixie and Hallie took their orders from Mrs. Belden, who was queen of her kitchen. Hallie set the table with the china and utensils that Trixie took from racks and drawers. Mr. Belden decided that Bobby would be more useful elsewhere and sent his youngest son in to work with Hallie. Bobby set the milk glasses in place. On the porch, the older boys raced to remove pale green husks while their father checked for brown silk threads still clinging to milky kernels.

Mrs. Belden called from the kitchen, "The water's boiling. Hurry!"

In rushed the cornhuskers. As fast as Mrs. Belden could rinse the ears in the sink, Brian popped the corn into the huge canning kettle. Over his shoulder, he said to Hallie, "Lucky you, to be here for the first corn of the season!"

"Do you grow corn in your garden?" Bobby asked.

Hallie whooped. "Are you kidding? I live in a mining town. Our crop is silver."

"Wow!" Bobby picked up a shining spoon and stared at his reflection. "This kind?"

"You betcha," Hallie said proudly.

Trixie didn't talk much while she sliced great red tomatoes. Thinking deeply, she tried to make sense of her violent reaction to Hallie's arrival. If she'd been working on a case, the days of Hallie's visit might have seemed less difficult to face. When Trixie was involved in tracking down clues, time always flew.

With or without company, just keeping her balance

during the coming three weeks was going to be almost more than Trixie could manage. For the first time, the Bob-Whites of the Glen were to take part in a wedding. Trixie was to be maid of honor when Jim's cousin, Juliana Maasden, married Hans Vorwald, a young attorney from Amsterdam.

Each time she thought of walking down the aisle, Trixie shivered nervously. Hallie couldn't have chosen a more inconvenient time to visit.

Trixie moved from one task to the next. She gave Mart the tomatoes to carry to the maple drop-leaf table. She reached for a silver tray and began arranging green onions, cucumbers, lettuce chunks, and tiny carrots. While she rummaged in the refrigerator for the radishes Bobby liked, something clicked in her mind. She popped a radish into her mouth and chewed noisily. "Bobby," she began, "what did you say about the mailbox?"

Warily he answered, "I said it's against the law to open other people's mailboxes."

"What about opening suitcases?" Mart put in slyly. He fished a carrot from Trixie's tray and got his fingers slapped. She offered him the plastic refrigerator bowl, and he helped himself to a radish.

Hallie told her worried young cousin, "Never mind, Bobby. I won't tell the police."

"Not that. I mean the part about the wheelchair," Trixie said.

"I dunno. Brian drove in front."

Brian was draining boiling water from the corn.

Holding his dark head well back from swirling steam, he said, "Now, that doesn't make sense. If there'd been a wheelchair for me to drive around, I'd have seen it. I drove around your scooter, Bobby."

"I didn't say you drove around it," Bobby said earnestly. "I said you drove in front and I couldn't see."

"Just where was the wheelchair, Bobby?" Trixie asked.

Bobby was tired of the conversation. "How do I know? I couldn't see it with my eyes. Just with the nocklers."

Mart wiggled sandy eyebrows at Bobby, then winked at Hallie. "Methinks it's a figment of the young lad's fertile imagination. He's a genius at getting out of a tight situation."

Bobby scowled. "I don't think I like what you sound like I said. Now can we eat, Moms?"

As she munched on sweet corn dripping with butter, Trixie worked on Bobby's puzzling statements. Once she asked, "Are you *sure* you saw a wheelchair?"

Bobby squirmed with impatience while Brian set the holders in the ends of a hot ear of corn. "Sure, I'm sure," he retorted as he began his third serving.

Off-Key Whistle • 3

HAVING EATEN so much corn that dessert would have to wait until later, the Beldens went about their business. Brian and Bobby took Hallie on a tour of the farm.

"Okay now, Trixie?" Mr. Belden asked casually. She nodded, and he carried the newspaper to the porch swing. Mrs. Belden joined him.

When Trixie began to clear the table, Mart offered, "You wash, I'll wipe."

While they worked, Trixie said, "I'm sorry I kicked you."

Mart grinned. He was exactly eleven months older than Trixie. Calling themselves the almost-twins, they often quarreled, but they also understood each other and were fiercely loyal.

"What kind of sense do you make of Bobby's story?" Trixie asked.

"None," Mart answered. "How could he have seen a wheelchair? Who do we know that owns one?"

Before she could think of an answer, Trixie heard the familiar sound of the Bob-White station wagon. She hurried to the back porch. As Jim Frayne slid out from behind the steering wheel, he called, "Did you save the pie?"

"We fought the good fight, but Moms protected that delectable concoction with her very life!" Mart shouted back. Jim, Honey, Di Lynch, and the young Beldens had picked raspberries all morning in anticipation of the evening treat.

Trixie met Honey with a hug. She waved a hello to red-haired Jim and watched as Hans and Juliana crossed the yard.

Tiny and blond, Juliana Maasden glowed with happiness, providing a sharp contrast with the injured girl who had recently regained her memory and health at Crabapple Farm. The solution of the mystery of Juliana's identity was considered by both Trixie and Honey to be one of their proudest achievements. They had proved Jim Frayne's dishonest stepfather to be the cause of the wreck that had almost cost Juliana both her life and her inheritance. And they had given Jim a gift he treasured above all others—a living relative.

Blowing kisses, Juliana ran across the drive and up the steps. As she jostled for space on the porch swing, Mr. Belden's paper slid off his lap. He woke with a start and rubbed a hand across his eyes. "Who's asleep? I was—"

"—just thinking with my eyes shut!" chorused Trixie and Honey.

Blond and tall, Hans leaned against a porch post. He shared the happy mood but said little. A rising young lawyer in Holland, he had come from Amsterdam to search for Juliana. His arrival had caused her to regain her memory. In August, he would take her home to Holland.

When all the guests were comfortable, Trixie took Honey to her room, then threw herself on one of the twin beds, arms flung wide. Dramatically she cried, "It's happened! She's here!"

Honey looked bewildered. "Who?"

Trixie scowled. "My cousin, Hallie Belden! That's who! I've told you about her."

"Oh! You mean the one you used to fight with."

"Exactly," Trixie said. "And because of her, I've already made one trip to the doghouse."

"What happened?" Honey asked sympathetically.

Trixie drew a deep breath. "You know me! I went charging around and got in trouble with Dad." Trixie rushed about her room, acting out her search for Hallie's missing clothing. Both girls collapsed on the bed closest to the window, giggling noisily. Then Trixie sobered. "But there is something unexplained.

37

Bobby says he saw somebody in a wheelchair."

From the doorway Bobby said, "That's wrong. I said I saw a wheelchair, and I said I saw somebody, but I didn't say I saw somebody *in* the wheelchair."

"Bobby!" Trixie shouted. "You know better than to enter a room without knocking!"

As reasonable as Trixie herself, Bobby argued, "I'm not in, and I couldn't knock on the door. It's open."

"So it is, Bobby," Honey agreed.

Growing more and more frustrated, Trixie said, "Well, if you didn't see anybody in the chair, maybe you didn't see it at all!"

"Wrong," Bobby declared. "I saw it, but Brian drove in front, so I couldn't see it anymore."

Trixie shook her short sandy curls. "He keeps saying that. 'Brian drove in front.' "

"Well, he did!" Bobby marched from the room.

From downstairs came moans and groans of sheer agony. Always hungry, Mart shouted, "When are we to partake of the well-earned succulence?" From porch and backyard came the answer, "Right now!"

Down on the porch, Trixie found that Brian had already introduced Hallie, who now sat on the steps between Jim and Bobby. Mart sprawled nearby, taking up space enough for two. "Hey!" he exclaimed. "There's space going to waste. Somebody's missing. I demand a roll call."

Honey teased, "As if you don't know who's absent, Mart Belden. Di's dad took the family out to dinner. He's going to drop Di off at our house on the way home so that she can spend the night. She wants to help with the wedding plans."

Mart pretended to pull spectacles to the end of his nose. "Thank you, Miss Wheeler. One must keep the record straight. One should know where one's compatriots are at all times. Consider—"

"I'd consider it more important to keep track of my enemies," Jim put in.

"In case their records aren't so straight?" Trixie asked.

Trixie saw that Hallie was watching and listening. Like the new child on a playground, Hallie wanted in on the activity, but she wasn't sure what game was being played. *Well*, Trixie thought, *I'm not sure I want her in the game!*

At that moment Trixie heard Juliana tell Mrs. Belden, "Just think. Soon I'll be Mrs. Hans Vorwald." Juliana wasn't playing a game. Her marriage would last "till death do us part."

Mrs. Belden patted Juliana's hand. "We'll miss you, dear."

"Until the wedding, you'll see me so often you'll be sick of the sight of me," Juliana said gaily.

Mart sagged in every muscle. "I agree, Juliana. For the want of a vision of beauty, I languish. Now, there are many kinds of beauty. For example, the smile on a youth's face when he contemplates a juicy berry pie—that's beauty beyond compare!"

"Okay, okay, I get it!" Trixie said. "You want to feed your face."

"Why didn't he just say so?" Hallie asked.

Amid the laughter, Trixie got up and went to the kitchen to cut Mrs. Belden's cobbler.

After the group was served, Trixie found that Jim had reserved space for her. She forgot the day's tensions as she and Jim enjoyed their pie together. Only when she heard Hallie chuckle was Trixie reminded that some changes had been made at the farm.

Honey stood and reached for Peter Belden's plate. "Everybody help clean up, then come home with us. We have wedding plans to talk about."

"I'll bring you Belden kids home," Jim promised.

"Okay, Moms?" Mart asked.

The Bob-Whites made a collective dash for the kitchen while Mrs. Belden called out, "Who waited to see if I said no?"

"Oh, Moms!" Trixie retorted over her shoulder. "You never do."

Hallie remained on the porch when the Bob-Whites, Hans, and Juliana crowded into the station wagon. "Get a move on, Hallie," Mart called.

Hallie made a helpless motion at her bare legs and feet. "Unless I put on my suit, I have nothing to wear. I can't go visiting dressed like this."

"You look fine to me," Jim told her.

Ordinarily, Trixie would share anything she owned with a friend, but she wasn't feeling exactly friendly toward Hallie. It took real effort for her to say to the others, "Wait for us. I'll find an outfit for Hallie."

Even in the dark, Honey sensed her effort. She

hugged Trixie and said, "Don't bother. Come on, Hallie. I'll find something for you in my closet. You're not much taller than I am."

As Hallie squeezed herself into the car, Mart teased, "Good thing you didn't take Trixie up on her magnanimous offer. You'd have had to borrow a belt from someone else." He groaned loudly when Trixie jabbed him with her finger. She was sensitive about weighing more than either Honey or Di, and Mart knew it. He reserved the right to remind her of this fact when he felt like getting even—and he hadn't forgotten the kick on his ankle, after all.

On Glen Road Jim caught sight of the Lynch Cadillac in his rearview mirror. He honked the horn and pulled to the side of the road to wait for Diana. No lengthy explanations were necessary as Di switched from roomy Cadillac to crowded station wagon. From the front seat, she twisted around to ask Honey, "May I borrow something comfortable to wear? I can't spend tonight and tomorrow, too, in these dressy clothes."

"You look super," Mart said. "Where did you eat?"

"The country club."

Mart crowed, "We, too, have indulged our taste buds."

"I know, with raspberry pie," Di said with a mock groan. "Remember me? I helped pick those berries." She affected a lofty air. "*We* had live entertainment. There was a stand-up comic."

"At the country club?" Jim asked in surprise.

"Some down-and-out actor was singing for his supper," Di explained. "He was really funny. He made everybody take part in an icebreaker. The host at each table introduced his group, then this character rushed around shouting introductions of all of us to people we'd known all our lives. And do you know what? He didn't miss a single name in that big dining room. He even remembered our addresses. And that was after he'd gone out for some reason, so some time had passed. I call that good!"

"See?" Mart grumbled. "Some people get *paid* for showing off memory skills! Other people languish for want of appreciation, not that I mention names."

"I thought that person languished for berry pie," Brian said dryly. "Di, we have a guest. Hallie Belden, Diana Lynch."

"Belden?" Di repeated. "Oh! Your cousin. Hi!"

There, Trixie thought. *One more Bob-White to go and Hallie will have met all of us.*

Jim drove past the gatehouse that now served as the Bob-White clubhouse. At the same time, the remaining unmet Bob-White, Dan Mangan, emerged from the woods path.

The station wagon came to a halt under a yard lamp. Trixie could hear Dan whistling off-key. He didn't sound happy. For several days, he had been unusually quiet. Trixie had tried to cheer him up, but Brian had told her to mind her own business. She had flared, "Dan's business *is* my business. He's a Bob-White, isn't he?" Quite pointedly, Brian had reminded her that each person is entitled to handle his own private affairs. Even though Dan now worked on the Wheeler estate, he was originally from the streets of New York City. Sleepyside-on-the-Hudson was situated close enough to the city that confrontations with his past were probably unavoidable. Brian would say nothing more.

As she led Hallie forward to meet Dan, Trixie studied his face for possible change. There was none. Dan still looked unhappy.

"Hi, Dan," Hallie said casually. She had two brothers and her tone said, "Big deal. Another boy."

But Dan's whole manner brightened. He fell into step with Hallie as if they'd walked together often.

As she had promised, Honey took the girls up to her room once they reached Manor House. There both Di and Hallie changed into comfortable jeans and blouses. "Am I presentable now?" Hallie asked.

"You're so pretty, Hallie, you'd look good in a gunnysack," answered Di. She locked arms with Hallie and guided her into the hall.

Trixie followed with Honey and Juliana. She watched the two dark-haired girls go down the wide stairs. It was an accepted fact that Di was the prettiest girl in the club. But now? Trixie was not so sure that even an Irish pixie with black hair and violet-colored eyes could compete with a girl who looked and walked like an Indian princess. If someone like Di took a backseat, what chance did Trixie have?

Miss Trask, housekeeper for the Wheelers and

friend to the Bob-Whites, was playing cards with Honey's parents and Mr. Lytell, who owned the grocery store on Glen Road. She welcomed Hallie warmly and drew her forward to meet the Wheelers and Mr. Lytell. Then the young people moved on into an alcove of the large room.

Trixie had been in charge of planning several large events, such as an antique show and an ice carnival. But a wedding? She was not sure exactly how much help Juliana needed or wanted. She listened to the Dutch girl's bubbling recital of plans already made. Trixie was to be maid of honor; Honey and Diana, bridesmaids; Brian, Mart, and Dan, ushers; and Bobby, ring bearer. "Di's twin sisters will be adorable flower girls," Juliana decided. "Jim—"

"Won't you escort the bride down the aisle, Jim?" Brian asked. "You're Juliana's only relative."

For a moment, Jim looked startled—this was growing up too fast! Then he reached across the space to his cousin's chair. He held both Juliana's tiny hands and said, "My dad has that honor. Since he adopted me, he's like an uncle to Juliana. I'm to be Hans's best man."

Hans smoothed very blond hair at one temple. Ruefully he said, "This wedding is beginning to sound complicated. We were to have had a simple civil ceremony in Amsterdam—no formality."

"That's still the way I want it," Juliana said. "I know Miss Trask has sent out a lot of invitations, but we can just put on our prettiest summer clothes and all meet here at Jim's house on the sixth of August. When our friends arrive, we'll simply take our places for the wedding ceremony. It will be no more trouble than receiving callers on a Sunday afternoon and will serve as a lovely good-bye party before we go home."

"If that pleases you, Juliana, then I am happy," Hans agreed.

Juliana turned eagerly to Hallie. "The Beldens were so kind to me during my illness that they became my second family. I can't leave out a Belden. Will you carry my guest book, Hallie?"

To Trixie's surprise, Hallie turned to her to ask, "Okay with you, Trix?"

"Wh-Why, sure," Trixie stammered. What else could she say? Jim had already shown how he felt about his cousin. That she might feel any less loving toward one of her own was something he simply wouldn't understand. It was a sobering thought.

After a short silence, Mart made an amusing story out of the suitcase mix-up. "Trixie tried to turn it into a full-fledged mystery, but that fell through. Now all we have left is that darned wheelchair Bobby says he saw."

Jim raised his head alertly and swung around to face Hans. "Say! That could have been a wheelchair we saw."

Hans was cautious. "I received only an impression. We were on a curve, meeting a car."

Trixie felt the familiar chill that was always her

response to mystery. She hugged herself, but goose bumps remained.

Mart noticed. "Oh, no!" he groaned. "Here we go again. Hans, Juliana, you'll just have to postpone those wedding plans till Trixie and Honey solve the mystery of the empty wheelchair!"

"Count me in, too," Hallie Belden drawled.

At that moment, Celia, the maid who was Miss Trask's right hand and also a friend of the Bob-Whites, crossed the large living room. She paused in the arch of the alcove and announced, "There's a telephone call for you, Diana. Your father."

"Dad?" Di was genuinely puzzled. As she followed Celia, she warned, "Don't talk till I get back. I don't want to miss a word."

The rugs were deep and soft, and no one heard Di return. It was Brian who looked up to find her standing in the archway. His instinctive concern for the mental and bodily welfare of people made him rise from his chair. "What's wrong? Are you all right?"

Di's hands lifted, then dropped. "I don't believe it," she said. "I just don't believe it."

Both Honey and Trixie went to her side.

"We've been robbed," Di said bleakly.

"Oh, that's a relief," Trixie blurted. "I thought someone was dead!"

"I—I'm sorry," Di said. "I didn't mean to scare you. I just don't believe it. There's nothing in our family room. Can you imagine it? Nothing!"

"You're kidding," Mart said flatly.

"I want to go home," Di said.

"I'll take you," Jim offered. "We'll all go."

For the moment, Trixie didn't think about a mystery to be solved. She only wanted to see Di smiling again.

The four-story Lynch mansion on the hill was lighted like a Christmas tree. Jim stopped in the turnaround at the entrance used by family and friends. It was on the side of the house directly opposite the formal entry. Here, a large foyer with a great stone fireplace was an extension of the family room. Jim, Honey, Brian, Mart, Hallie, Dan, Di, and Trixie marched in single file through the door, across the foyer, and into the family room, as orderly as a column of ants. Although the thick carpeting muffled their footsteps, they all tiptoed.

"There's—nothing here!" Mart exclaimed.

"That's what I told you," Di reminded him.

"If they could have carried the fireplace away, they would have," Dan said. After a quick, nervous inspection of the room, he returned to the foyer. He stared into the cavernous mouth of the fireplace, unused since spring, and suddenly stooped to pick up a small wad of paper. Several times he tossed the paper into the air and caught it. The action made Trixie uneasy. That dark, unhappy look was on Dan's face again.

The next time Dan tossed the wad of paper, Trixie caught it and rolled it between her fingers. It didn't feel like the gum wrapper she had thought it to be.

Because she wasn't used to an empty room in this luxurious home, Trixie was glad to have something to do. She unrolled the paper wad. The paper was of good quality and didn't tear. When she saw words written on the paper, Trixie flinched as if she'd been caught opening another person's mail. Then she saw the familiar crest of the Sleepyside Country Club. A bubble of excitement grew in her throat and burst into words. "Look! It's your address, Di!"

"So? We live here," Di said.

"But it's written on country club paper, and it says, 'Early. Kids.' "

"What's this about early kids?" a voice asked from the end of the foyer. Di's father, followed by Sergeant Molinson, the policeman from Sleepyside, joined the young people, who wandered aimlessly about the foyer and family room.

Although her bump of curiosity itched painfully, Trixie knew she couldn't withhold evidence from the police. She handed the crumpled paper to the sergeant. "Dan found this in the fireplace."

"I noticed it because it was lodged against the glass fireguard," Dan explained. "It—well, it was just the only thing in the room!"

"Except for the drapes and carpet," Di corrected.

Trixie looked at the blank walls. Even the pictures and games were gone from the walls.

The policeman took the paper, turned it over, then waved it to catch Mr. Lynch's attention. "What do you make of this, sir? Is this your handwriting?"

Where's Di's Invitation? • 4

MR. LYNCH TOOK the crumpled paper from Sergeant Molinson. "No, I didn't write this, but I recognize the paper. I'm a director at the club. This sheet is from one of the note pads we place at the telephones there. Anybody can use them. That's what they're for."

The sergeant nodded. "I suppose this could be a confirmation of your dinner reservation. You took your whole family to dinner tonight, as I understand it."

"That's right," Mr. Lynch said, "but I can't see this message as fitting the situation. At the club, my name and reservation time would have been listed with the

number of guests to be at my table. Here at home—
well, I can't imagine Harrison unbending enough to
use the word 'kids.'"

Harrison was the prim and proper butler who managed the Lynch household. He had been with the
family since their sudden rise to wealth. At one time,
while they were getting used to their new life-style,
Mrs. Lynch had fired both him and the children's
nurses. Coping with the huge house had proved so
overwhelming that they had all been rehired. Harrison was now as much of an institution there as Miss
Trask was at Manor House. And it was unthinkable
that he would either say or write "kids."

"Sergeant Molinson—" Trixie began.

"Yes, Detective Belden?" The sergeant didn't try
to hide his amusement. "I wondered how long it
would take you to get into the act."

"Could the thief have written that note?" Trixie
asked with a rush.

"Dim-witted thief!" Mart snorted. "That letterhead
practically gives his address. All the police have to do
is interview the staff at the club to find out who was
off tonight."

"Oh." Trixie was stymied, but only briefly. "Maybe
he is a dumb kind of thief, or an inexperienced one."

"I don't buy that," the sergeant said. "This is obviously the work of several people who knew exactly
what they were doing. A truck was driven right to the
door for loading. The tracks on the turnaround are
still visible, and Harrison says he met a truck on the

private road that leads down to Glen Road. That would indicate a lookout was on the job. Dumb thieves probably, but not inexperienced."

"What happened, Dad?" Di asked unhappily.

The story was brief. Because it was the cook's birthday, Mr. Lynch had arranged for the whole staff to celebrate at Glen Road Inn. He had taken his own family to the country club. Shortly before the family's arrival home, the servants had returned to find the foyer and family room stripped of furniture.

"Somebody must have tipped off this gang that you'd be home early because you had taken the children," the sergeant decided.

Mr. Lynch's jolly laugh rumbled in spite of the circumstances. "If you had two sets of twins, you'd bring them home early, too, Sergeant."

The sergeant agreed. As he left the house he said, "I'll keep in touch. You'll have your insurance man make out a list of the missing articles?"

"Right." Mr. Lynch closed the heavy foyer door. He asked Di's friends if they wanted to walk through the house to see if anything else was missing.

Bright-eyed with interest, Trixie led the exploration of the first floor. Everything seemed in its usual formal order. In Di's home, one didn't leave jackets on chairs, tennis rackets on tables, or apple cores in ashtrays. Harrison managed a "tight ship," with each set of twins cared for by its own nurse. Not even the country club had a more efficient staff. Each time she was in this mansion, Trixie realized how much she

51

appreciated the comfortable freedom of her own pleasant and informal home.

Several times Jim looked at his wristwatch. At last he said, "If there's nothing else we can do to be of help here, Di, I think we'd better go. It's late."

"I know," Di agreed. "Thank you for bringing me home. Honey, I'll stay with you some other night."

As Jim drove down the winding private road, Trixie looked back at the fully lighted house. She heard Dan mutter, "Nobody is going to sleep well at that house tonight." It puzzled Trixie that he sounded so angry.

The next morning, Trixie dressed the minute she awoke and quickly ran down the lane to pick up the morning paper. She found that Mart was at the box ahead of her, with the pages of the *Sleepyside Sun* opened out like the sails of a boat.

Mart called, "Hi, twin," then announced, "Those thieves were busy little beavers last night. Besides pulling the Lynch robbery, they entered a house on Bowling Green but were chased out by a dog named Manchu. They took everything of value from a house near Glen Road Inn, and they totally stripped one of those new houses down on the river." Mart read aloud, " 'Police report the common denominator is the fact that the owners of all these properties dined last night at the Sleepyside Country Club, attracted by the performance of the comic, Oliver Tolliver.' "

Mart chewed his lip. "If I were that Oliver Tolliver, I'd be moving on."

"What? Oh, I see," said Trixie. "His name is linked with a police report, and that's bad publicity."

"Right," Mart agreed. "Want to share the paper?"

"Too late. Here comes Dad," Trixie said. "Do the police know the order of the robberies?"

"They're guessing. Sergeant Molinson built a time-table based on telephoned information."

"Got in pretty late last night" was Mr. Belden's greeting.

"Boy, was there a reason!" Mart said. "It's spread all over the front page of the *Sun*."

Together Trixie and Mart began to tell their story and managed to confuse Peter Belden totally. He begged, "Kindly let me read it for myself, please."

When the three reached the kitchen, they found Brian and Hallie telling Mrs. Belden and Bobby about the empty family room at the Lynch mansion.

"You mean, somebody tooked—I mean, taked—"

"How about just plain *took*, Bobby?" Mrs. Belden corrected.

"—just plain took all those neat games in the playroom?" Bobby asked.

"Every one," Trixie told him.

"Even Di's portable radio shaped like a doughnut?" Bobby persisted.

"That, too," Mart agreed.

"Boy," Bobby mourned, "that's sad. I liked that radio. Di was going to let me hang it on the handle-bar of my bike. If I ever get a bike."

"That's nice, Bobby." Mr. Belden winked solemnly,

53

then ducked behind his newspaper to hide a grin.

"No," Bobby declared. "It isn't nice at all. The radio is just plain took. Now I can't borrow it."

Trixie thought of all the hours of fun she had shared in that family room at the Lynch mansion. "It is sad, Bobby. I'm sorry the radio was 'just plain took.'"

Only Trixie and Hallie sat with Mr. Belden while he drank his second cup of coffee. They were faced by the printed wall of his propped-up newspaper. All they could see were the want ads.

"Need your gutters cleaned?" Hallie droned. "Interested in self-hypnosis? Swimming lessons? Wrecking service?"

Trixie broke in. "Listen to this! 'Lost: Wheelchair. Vicinity Lytell Store on Glen Road. Reward. Call Teed Moving Service.'"

Hallie wrinkled her straight nose. "So that's what happened. A wheelchair rolled out of a truck."

Trixie shrugged and reached for more toast. "There goes our mystery." She snapped her fingers. "Gleeps! We can try for the reward money anyway. With the wedding coming up, the Bob-Whites can use extra money. When Moms lets me out of the kitchen, I'll look for the wheel marks. That wheelchair didn't just land beside the road like a helicopter."

Hallie grinned. "Count me in." Trixie agreed unwillingly.

She felt more cheerful when Hallie offered to dust. It was a chore Trixie hated.

Wearing a pair of Trixie's shorts and a knit shirt,

Hallie padded barefoot to the end of the lane with Trixie. The Belden mailbox stood in a clump of daisies. "No marks," Trixie muttered.

"What did you expect?" Hallie retorted. "The mail truck's stopped here. Brian's jalopy's gone up the lane. Uncle Peter's come and gone. I don't see any marks farther up the road, either. Could Bobby have seen somebody else's mailbox?"

Trixie looked toward the Belden house in the valley. She studied its height and the placement of her window. Out of sight beyond a strip of forestland lay the Wheeler estate with its many buildings. In that short distance to Manor House, several mailboxes served people, like Mr. Maypenny and Tom and Celia Delanoy, who lived off the county road. Hidden on a hilltop in the distance stood Di Lynch's large stone home. It was visible only in winter when the trees were bare. Their mile-long private road twisted downhill to Glen Road, where their mailbox stood at the intersection. The Frayne mansion had burned, so that property had no use for a box. Mr. Lytell's store couldn't be seen.

Trixie sighed. "No, I can't see mailboxes from my window. Not even our own."

"Well, neither could Bobby without binoculars."

To cover a feeling of pique that Hallie had made a point, Trixie opened the mailbox. She drew out five heavy white envelopes, each addressed in Miss Trask's perfect script.

"Our invitations!" Trixie's voice softened with the

wonder of holding proof in her hand that Juliana and Hans were to be married, and that Trixie Belden was to be maid of honor. "Look. Here's a separate invitation for Bobby. They knew he'd like one for a souvenir." Waving her fan of white envelopes, she ran up the lane shouting, "Mail! It's important!"

In the backyard, Trixie dealt out the mail, then ran into the house to call Honey.

In the window seat at the end of the upstairs hall, Trixie dialed the familiar number. While the call went through, she propped the receiver on her shoulder and opened the outer envelope. She wiped her warm fingers on her shorts before pulling the engraved invitation from the second envelope. There were the magic words:

> Mr. and Mrs. Matthew Wheeler
> request the honor of your presence
> at the marriage of
> Juliana Maasden
> to
> Mr. Hans Vorwald,
> on Friday, the sixth of August,
> at half after four o'clock,
> at the Manor House,
> Glen Road,
> Sleepyside-on-the-Hudson, New York.

Suddenly Trixie became aware of Honey saying over and over again, "Hello? Hello?"

"Hello, Honey!" Trixie squealed. "I'm reading it, Honey. I'm reading my invitation, and it's beautiful! Is Juliana up yet?"

"Oh, my goodness, yes! She and Hans are down by the sundial looking at travel folios. Anyway, that's what they're doing when they're not just holding hands and looking at each other." Honey laughed softly. "They think they're out of sight of the whole world, but they're not. I can look right down into that part of the garden, where Miss Trask had all the old-fashioned flowers planted this year."

For the briefest of moments, Trixie had a vision of Bobby looking into some secret glade from a second-floor window at Crabapple Farm. She told herself she had wheelchair on the brain. "See you later, Honey. I'm going to call Di. I'll talk to Juliana later."

"Tell Di that the Bob-Whites are invited here for lunch. We'll swim first."

It took several minutes to reach Diana. Harrison took the call. He relayed the message to a maid before Di was located and answered the phone.

"Di, isn't it wonderful?" Trixie sang out. "This is the very first wedding invitation I ever got. I've been included before with the family, of course, but. . . ." Brows knitted, Trixie listened to uneven breathing sounds. Was Di crying? Guiltily Trixie realized that her excitement about the invitation had momentarily wiped out the memory of the trouble at Di's house.

"Oh, Di! I'm sorry I rattled on like that. Is something else wrong? Did the robbers come back?"

Di sniffled. Then she said very quietly, "We're fine. The robbers didn't come back. Mother and Dad got an invitation, but I didn't."

"Di!" Trixie gasped. "There's some mistake."

"I didn't get one," Di repeated stiffly.

"Please don't be like that, Di," Trixie begged. "Let me call Honey and tell her what happened. You've addressed Christmas cards. You know how easy it is to skip a name on the list."

"Well . . . yes," Di agreed reluctantly.

"Honey says we're invited there for lunch," Trixie added.

"If she wants me, she can call me."

"Oh, Di!" Trixie wailed. The minute she heard Di hang up, Trixie dialed Honey's number again. This time Honey was not in her room.

The maid, Celia, was making beds and told Trixie to call the stable. "Honey is exercising Lady and Starlight."

Trixie knew that meant Jim was handling Jupiter, Strawberry, and Susie, the small black mare reserved for Trixie's own use.

Usually the young Beldens helped with the stable work in exchange for the privilege of riding the Wheeler horses at any time they chose. But due to their work at home, they hadn't been to the stable for some days. Even Bobby was helping harvest the raspberries at Crabapple Farm. Trixie had been excused this one day only because it was the first full day of Hallie's visit. There simply was no time for the horses, in spite of the coming Turf Show.

Regan, the groom, wouldn't like this interruption of the horses' exercise, but he'd certainly understand if he knew Di's feelings were hurt. Regan and Miss Trask were the Bob-Whites' best friends. Trixie made the call to the stable.

Again she had to wait. The chauffeur, Tom, answered. He shouted to Regan, who used his megaphone to call in Honey.

Breathlessly Honey asked, "Is something wrong, Trixie? Didn't Celia tell you that I—"

"She told me," Trixie said briefly. "Honey, something awful has happened. Di didn't get an invitation, and she's been crying."

"Oh!" Tenderhearted Honey drew a quivering breath of dismay. "There's some mistake. I know Di was sent an invitation. I'll call the house and have Miss Trask send another, right this minute. Di's had enough trouble. We can't allow her to be hurt. We simply can't! I have to get back to the horses now. See you at lunch."

Even with a guest in the house and other people's troubles on her mind, Trixie had work to do. To her surprise, Hallie worked hard. "I thought you had maids," Trixie said.

Hallie shrugged. "One. But you know my parents. Slave drivers!"

"It runs in the Belden family," Trixie retorted, as naturally as if she were working with Honey herself.

On one of his many trips to the cooler with berries,

Brian called Miss Trask. He asked her to excuse Mart and himself from lunch at Manor House. They both felt they should spend as much time as possible picking berries.

Having prepared lunch for the stay-at-home Beldens, Trixie and Hallie biked up Glen Road. They rode slowly, watching for narrow wheel marks in the dust beside the road. About halfway between the lane and the Manor House turnoff, they saw something that made them start. A young, nearly bald man was pushing an empty wheelchair toward them.

"Gleeps! That's our wheelchair!" Trixie exclaimed.

Hallie shrugged. "So what? He found it first."

Trying not to feel disappointed, Trixie said, "No sense calling Teed Moving Service now."

"No wheelchair, no reward," Hallie agreed.

"And no mystery," Trixie added. But if that were true, why did she have the uneasy feeling that this man wished he hadn't been seen? As they came face-to-face, she noticed a look of softness about the man that Mart would have called sissiness. Still, he was a broad-shouldered, rather tall man, clean-shaven and ordinary-looking.

Trixie glanced back several times. Once she caught the man looking back at her.

Again a prickle of uneasiness caused Trixie to scan the road. Glen Road itself had a hard surface and yielded little in the way of clues. But, there, some distance before the Wheeler mailbox, a wilted clematis vine lay across the edge of the road.

A Disturbing Phone Call · 5

TRIXIE BRAKED HER BICYCLE for a closer look at the wilted vine. This could be the spot where Jim and Hans had seen the chair. There was room for a wheelchair to have been hidden among those dusty bushes.

On the other hand, last night's fleeing thieves could have bruised the clematis. After a close look, both Hallie and Trixie agreed they could see no truck tire marks beyond the traffic lane, nor could they find wheelchair marks.

Beside the Wheeler mailbox, Di waited for the cousins. She looked so sober that Trixie decided not to mention either the robbery or the missing invitation unless she had to. She was glad to talk about the mystery that was no mystery. "That man must have found the chair yesterday and shoved it out of the way of traffic. When he read his paper, he came back for the reward."

Di made no response. After a tactful silence, Hallie raised the possibility that two men could have been involved. In any case, she still wondered how Bobby could have seen a man from that upstairs window the day before.

When they reached the clubhouse, they found that Jim and Honey had already changed into bathing suits. Dan rode up on Spartan. As he came closer, he began an off-key whistle. Spartan had been a circus horse and responded to the melody with a ponderous dance. Hallie applauded the performance enthusiastically.

Dan was so obviously pleased by Hallie's reaction that Trixie didn't mind—much—when Jim walked to the lake with her cousin. It gave her a chance to walk with Honey. That left Dan with Di, and Trixie heard him ask, "Your dad had insurance on your furniture, didn't he?"

"Oh, sure," Di answered, "but it's difficult to make an exact list of everything that was in the room last night—like my doughnut-shaped portable radio. I'm pretty sure it was in the family room yesterday. I never leave it on my bike handle, and there's no sense carrying it to my room. I have a stereo up there."

"I'm sorry, Di. If I could have prevented this. . . ." Dan's voice dwindled to a mumble. Trixie wondered how on earth Dan thought he could have prevented that robbery.

By the time they reached the dock at the lake, Di was almost cheerful again, and so was Dan.

Lunch at Manor House was served at a large round picnic table set on the flagstone area near a very old birdbath. Black-faced cardinals sang, "Wet year, wet year, weet, weet, weet!" Dan found a couple of melon seeds in his fruit cup and flipped them out to the birds. This started the whole red-feathered flock strutting around the table, looking for more handouts. Even Mr. Wheeler hunted for stray seeds and sent Jim to the kitchen to rescue some from the garbage disposal.

In this gay setting, Hans glowed each time he looked at Juliana, and so did Jim. Once Jim turned to Trixie to say, "There's something special about knowing that another person has the same ancestry as you do."

Again Trixie was reminded that Jim wouldn't understand her wariness toward Hallie—the wariness that she was trying so hard to conceal. She had to admit that Hallie was easier to get along with than she had expected.

In a fresh white pants suit loaned by Honey, Hallie looked relaxed and totally at home. She didn't stand in awe of Honey's parents. Trixie heard her ask their red-haired host, "Are you sure Jim is adopted?"

Mr. Wheeler touched his red sideburns as he grinned at red-haired, freckled Jim. "I'm sure, but we don't advertise it, not with our carrottops."

At that moment, Celia brought the garden telephone to the table. "Excuse me, Mrs. Wheeler. There's a call for Mr. Hans."

"Would you like to take the call over by the birdbath?" Mrs. Wheeler asked her guest.

With a quick little bow that included everyone at the table, Hans took the phone from Celia. He walked across the grass to sit on the edge of the birdbath. Trixie was facing him. She saw him straighten suddenly and turn his back to the table. His whole pose was that of a person being presented with a problem. Trixie glanced at Juliana but saw that she had not noticed.

Juliana was asking permission to be driven to Sleepyside by Tom, the chauffeur. Her own blue Volkswagen was being repaired as a result of the wreck that had caused her loss of memory for a time.

"I'll drive you, Juliana," Jim offered.

Juliana giggled. "I'm afraid you'll be bored with my window-shopping, Jim." She smiled brightly as Hans returned to the table. "Tell Jim, Hans, what a slowpoke I am when I shop."

"She's the worst," Hans agreed indulgently, "but I have good arches." Reseated, he picked up his napkin and asked, "By the way, Juliana, was your family on friendly terms with some people named Ryks?"

"I—I'm sure I don't know," Juliana answered. "I was very young when the accident took both my parents. When the Schimmels took me in, their friends became my friends. Among them I can't recall the name Ryks. Is it important?"

"It seemed important to the Miss Ryks who telephoned," Hans told her. He shook his blond head as if to clear away cobwebs. "Do you know, now that I try to reconstruct her conversation, I am not clear as to whether she considers herself a friend of my family or yours?"

"Does it matter?" Juliana asked gaily. "In a few days, there won't be any difference. Your family will be *my* family."

Miss Trask asked, "May I help, Hans?"

"Thank you, Miss Trask," Hans said. "This person who called from the Glen Road Inn has asked if it is possible for her to be included on the guest list for our wedding."

Honey's mother lifted both hands and let them drop as if she emptied them of all responsibility, as, indeed, she did on every possible occasion. "My dear Miss Trask, whatever you decide is quite all right."

Miss Trask leaned across the table to speak with Jim. "Since you two are related, it's conceivable that your two families might have had friends in common. Do you recall the name Ryks?"

"No," Jim said soberly. "I'm sharing the boat with Juliana. I have no strong link with the past. My mother remarried after my father's death. You all know how that turned out. Being a friend of my stepfather is a poor recommendation."

"Well, let me call the inn and see what I can find

out," Miss Trask said. "Is that agreeable with you, Hans? Juliana?" Both agreed.

As a signal that their young guests were free to do as they chose, Honey's parents left the table to walk through the well-kept grounds.

Before any more of the group left, Trixie reminded everyone that they were invited to Crabapple Farm for dinner that evening. The get-together had been planned a week earlier.

"We'll be there. Now let's drop off your bikes at Crabapple Farm and then all go to Sleepyside with Juliana," Honey said eagerly.

Dan asked to be excused to return to work. As he left the terrace, he looked back. Trixie knew he would rather have remained with his friends.

There were several nice shops in Sleepyside, small village though it was. Customers included the wealthy owners of the estates lining the Hudson. Trixie, Honey, Hallie, and Di trooped from counter to counter, helping Juliana to make choices. Jim and Hans carried packages. Several times Trixie saw them in sober conversation. When curiosity got the better of her, she asked Jim if he'd like a break.

"Sure. Hans, let's take the packages to the car."

Juliana objected prettily. "I'm not quite finished here, Hans."

"Jim, you and Trixie go ahead," Honey urged. "We'll meet you later."

After they had locked the packages in the station

wagon in the village parking lot, Trixie and Jim walked the short distance to Wimpy's. They waved at the counterboy and hurried to their favorite booth. "Root beer—a tall one, please," Trixie ordered.

"Make it two," Jim added.

When their frosted mugs came, Trixie waited impatiently for Jim to tell her what was on his mind. Like Bobby, Jim couldn't be hurried. She filled him in on the story of the wheelchair, but he listened with only part of his attention. He cut in to say, "That phone call worries Hans."

"I don't see why it should bother him," Trixie said. "It was a local call. Glen Road Inn can't be more than a couple of miles from Manor House."

"It isn't even that far," Jim corrected. "That's the part that worries Hans. He doesn't know anyone in the valley, and Juliana doesn't know anyone we don't know. Hans thinks it's strange that Miss Ryks didn't call when Juliana was in trouble, if she's all that much of a friend of the family. On the other hand, if Miss Ryks just arrived at the inn, how did she know where to find Juliana? And why did she ask for Hans, not Juliana?"

"It is confusing, isn't it?" Trixie agreed. Her logical mind began working on the problem. "Juliana went to college in New York. I'm sure she knows lots of people. There are her special friends, the De Jongs, on vacation in the Poconos. Any number of people could have told Miss Ryks where to find Juliana. Her close friends know about her engagement to Hans.

By this time, they're getting their wedding invitations. Word must be getting around."

Jim nodded. "I suppose it's even possible that Miss Ryks knows some other Hans Vorwald."

"Who's engaged to some other Juliana Maasden?" Trixie teased. "Since Vorwald and Maasden are such very ordinary names, that has to be the answer!"

Jim forced a smile. He picked up and set down his mug several times, making a pattern of wet rings.

"Is there something you're not telling me, Jim?" Trixie asked.

"No. It's only that Hans would just as soon forget that phone call, but it was such a strange call that he can't."

"And neither can you," Trixie sighed. The chill she felt was not caused by drinking frosted root beer.

A small sporting goods store stood across the street from Wimpy's. In muggy, end-of-July weather, the shop didn't do much business. That was the first reason that Trixie noticed a man stop to look at its one display window. The second reason was that she was sure she had seen that same man, just a few hours earlier, pushing an empty wheelchair down Glen Road.

She became so absorbed in watching him that she walked over to a window to get a better view. Jim followed. He studied the whole block. "What in blazes do you see out there, Trixie?"

"Let's go look at that display window."

For the first time since they had talked about Hans's

strange phone call, Jim Frayne laughed. "It takes a mind reader to keep up with you, Trixie." He paid for their root beers and followed her out the door.

It was like stepping from an icebox into an oven, but Trixie ignored the heat and marched across the street. When she reached the store window, she gazed inside a moment, then muttered, "Nuts!"

"Well, what did you expect? Cannonballs?"

Inside the shop, the tall young man bent over a showcase. He pointed at a gun so small that it looked as harmless as a toy. Jim whistled. "Wow! That's a wicked one. With a little work, its trigger can be set to go off if you blow on it. Now, why do you suppose he wants that?"

"He doesn't," Trixie answered. "He's buying rope." As she started to turn from the window, the man glanced up. For a long moment he stared, then bowed. Trixie nodded in return.

In surprise Jim asked, "Do you know him?"

"Do you?" Trixie countered. "He's looking at you, too." She caught sight of Honey, already inside Wimpy's and waving for their attention. "Come on. We're being paged."

Following her, Jim said, "You never did answer my question, Trixie."

"About that man? He's the one Hallie and I saw pushing that wheelchair. He must have collected the reward money, and it's burning a hole in his pocket."

Trixie and Jim had stood in the sun long enough to get thirsty again. They reordered root beers and joined in the talk about everything and nothing. Trixie sketched the latest news about the wheelchair.

Suddenly Hallie said, "I saw a truck go by."

"How about that? Don't they have trucks in Idaho?" Jim teased. "Now, let me tell you about trucks. They're vehicles, four-wheeled, used for—"

Hallie ignored Jim. "This was a truck belonging to the Teed Moving Service—the same moving service that lost the wheelchair."

"Where?" Trixie tried to scan the street from her place in the middle of the group.

Hallie jerked a thumb toward the parking lot. "In the alley."

"I never noticed a warehouse there," Trixie said.

Jim asked, "Why should you? What have you wanted to have hauled that wouldn't go in the station wagon?" He shrugged. "I suppose you want to go over there."

"Why not?" Trixie demanded. "We can just kind of. . . ." She gestured with both hands, palms up, as if she weighed invisible objects.

Honey giggled. "All right. Let's go, 'kind of.'"

While shopping bags were stored in the station wagon, Jim suggested that it might look odd if the whole group inquired about one wheelchair. He told Trixie, "We'll wait for you."

Trixie pulled Honey across the parking lot on the run while Hallie loped two steps behind.

Teed Moving Service occupied a warehouse on an alley behind Wimpy's. When the three girls entered, they found no one behind the high counter that blocked off an office area. A desk sign read, HATTIE ROE. Two men, wearing visored caps with badges, leaned elbows on the counter. One of them said, "Hattie's out back somewhere for a few minutes," then turned back to resume his conversation.

"The darnedest thing happened on my run yesterday. I was supposed to deliver this wheelchair to a cripple, see, out near where all them rich guys live—Wheelers, Lynches, Beldens—and—"

Trixie sputtered. This was the first time she had ever heard her family called rich. For an instant, she worried about the ethics of eavesdropping. *But,* she argued with herself, *how can I be eavesdropping when they're looking right at me while they talk?* They had to be talking about that intriguing wheelchair! But—who was crippled?

"Well, here's what happened, see. Hattie musta wrote down a wrong number. I told her I never heard of no such place out there, and I was right, 'cause when I found that address it belonged to a burnt-out shell of a house with weeds growing through the bricks."

Honey whispered, "Jim's uncle's house." Trixie nodded. The Frayne house had burned.

"Just in case they'd built a house back in the woods someplace, I got out and scouted around, see, but there wasn't no house, just like I told Hattie. All I could do was get back in the pickup with this guy I'd given a lift. He was sittin' there waitin' for me."

71

"That's a violation," the second driver reminded the storyteller.

"Sure, but I figured old man Teed wouldn't never find out. I chalked it up to a public service.

"Well, I let this guy off down the road, and I turned off on a side road to finish my deliveries, see. When I got back here to report in, I didn't have no wheelchair, and I didn't have no signed, sealed, and delivered slip neither. Now, what d'ya make of that?"

"Tough luck," the second man muttered. "Trouble?"

"Well—I dunno. Not yet. Teed, he put an ad in the *Sun* and I'm waitin' to ask Hattie if that chair got turned in. She takes all the phone calls. She oughta know. Wish me luck. Here she comes."

Silently both the drivers and the girls watched Hattie Roe, the desk clerk, return to her post. She told the drivers, "I'll talk to you in a minute." She asked the girls, "May I help you?"

"It's about the wheelchair," Hallie said, leaving Trixie with her mouth open, her question unasked.

Hattie tapped the eraser of her pencil against the counter. "Are you the folks who ordered that chair from White Plains Hospital Supply? There seems to have been a mix-up. If you'll give me the right address, I'll see that the matter is taken care of."

"No," Hallie explained, "we didn't order it. We noticed your ad in the paper, and we just want to report that we saw the chair."

By this time, Trixie was sizzling. Here stood the Belden-Wheeler Detective Agency in person—*both* persons!—without a chance to get a word in edgewise. Who did Hallie Belden think she was?

"On Glen Road," Trixie put in sharply.

Hattie glanced at Trixie, but she spoke to Hallie. "Thank you for your interest. That chair was returned." She nodded toward the drivers.

The man in trouble mopped his brow and said, "Looks like I'm off the hook." Both drivers walked through a door marked EMPLOYEES ONLY.

Feeling both let down and angry, Trixie headed for the station wagon. The faster she walked, the angrier she became. At her heels and breathing down her neck came Hallie. Behind Hallie, Honey made placating noises meant to calm both cousins.

When they reached the car, Hallie made a flat statement. "That was sure a wild-goose chase. Ever since I came, I've heard nothing but wheelchair, wheelchair. Now we can forget about it. If that man's a criminal, he's got holes in his head. All his secrets are spread out in plain sight."

Several times during this speech, Trixie tried to break in. Finally she exclaimed loudly, "Hallie Belden! You were the one who saw the truck!"

Hallie shrugged. "So I saw a pickup."

"And who asked all the questions? You did!"

Hallie grinned. "So I've got a big mouth."

With her temper bouncing like corn in a popper and no Brian present to cool her down, Trixie yelled, "If you had sense enough to keep track of your own belongings, nobody would have seen a wheelchair!

I suppose it's going to be like this all the rest of the summer. Whenever I turn around, there *you* are, causing me trouble!"

In case Hallie wasn't hearing well, Trixie shouted. "If you didn't think there was something fishy about this wheelchair business, why did you horn in?"

Abruptly Trixie became aware of silence and watchful eyes. Jim was the only one not staring. He was fumbling with his ignition key. While Trixie gulped down her temper, Jim walked around the hood of the wagon and held open the door. He didn't look at Trixie.

Trixie didn't move. In one of her rare outbursts, Honey cried, "For goodness' sake, we all have work to do. Let's go home and do it!"

Feeling guilty and foolish, Trixie joined Di and Hallie in the backseat. Already frightened by the robbery and hurt by the missing invitation, Di was very upset by Trixie's display. She asked the others' opinions about this and that, and nothing she said made much sense. Trixie didn't talk, even when Hans tried to be polite to her.

When Jim drove up the farm lane, Trixie couldn't scramble out of the car fast enough. Nervously she told the others, "Don't be late for dinner. H-Hallie and I are cooking tonight, aren't we, Hallie?"

"Sure," Hallie agreed, sealing a hasty truce.

Scooped · 6

Before they entered the house, Trixie and Hallie shook hands. Each muttered, "I'm sorry," then went straight to the kitchen and set to work.

In less than five minutes, however, Trixie exclaimed, "I still feel like hitting something!"

"How about a tennis ball?" Hallie asked, half joking.

Trixie was struck by sudden inspiration. "We don't have a court, just the net in the backyard. Are you game to bike to the country club for a real set?"

Hallie shrugged. "Okay. How far is it?"

"It's downhill coming home," Trixie hedged.

Luckily they didn't have to pedal far. Before they

reached Mr. Lytell's store, they heard a car behind them. Di's father slowed his Cadillac to shout, "Going my way?"

"Country club?" Trixie shouted back.

"Righto. Hop in. I'll put your bikes in the trunk." As soon as they were seated, he launched into a recital about the news item in the *Sun*. He ended by saying, "There's the darnedest development for the club directors to handle, too. That stand-up comic at the club has quit."

"Mart thought he might," Trixie said slowly.

"Smart boy, Mart. If he could pack 'em in like that fellow Tolliver, we'd hire him!"

"Did the police find out who wrote that note in the fireplace?" Hallie asked.

"Nobody at our house, or else our own telephone notepaper would have been used. It matches the decor, you know."

Trixie grinned. "Royal blue and gold."

"My wife's a nut about having things match," Mr. Lynch said. "Even children!" He roared at his own joke about the two sets of twins at his house.

Before going to the tennis courts, Trixie stopped at the nearest club telephone and looked at the note pad to see for herself that Mr. Lynch was right. The note in the fireplace did match this paper.

Trixie found that she had to work when she faced Hallie across the net. The younger girl had strong legs and a smashing serve. They had long since forgotten their argument when Mr. Lynch plopped down on a spectators' bench. "Thought you two might like a ride home."

By the time the Belden family was under one roof again, the girls were working together, if not happily, at least calmly.

Dinner that second night of Hallie's visit was a gathering of the Bob-Whites, Hans, and Juliana. Even Dan Mangan was there. Not usually vain about his appearance, Dan had trimmed the sideburns of his long dark hair for this occasion. Instead of the "tough guy" black clothing he used to wear, he was neatly dressed in faded jeans and a denim jacket. Trixie thought he looked nice and told him so. He grinned and went in search of Hallie.

When the table was cleared for dessert, Hans excused himself. From the Belden refrigerator, he brought a corsage of tiny white rosebuds. When he sat at the table again, he gave the flowers to Honey and said, "Pass it on."

As each person looked at the corsage, Trixie heard whispers: "Oh, my!" "Lovely." "Perfect!"

Unable to control her curiosity another minute, Trixie asked, "What's so special about roses?" When it was her turn to receive the flowers, she saw what was so special. Fastened with a wisp of white ribbon, Juliana's engagement ring circled one tiny rosebud.

"Oh-h," Trixie breathed. From the land where diamond cutting was a fine art had come this old, old ring—a cluster of perfect diamonds set in the center of a delicate golden tulip. When the corsage reached

Juliana, Hans took it from her hand. He untied the ribbon and placed the ring on Juliana's finger.

"That ring's too big," Bobby piped.

Hans smiled. "We'll have it altered to fit, Bobby."

Wisely Bobby advised, "You can put it in hot water and shrink it. That's what Trixie did to my sweater."

"That's our Trixie!" Mart hooted.

Dan explained, "You don't shrink gold, Bobby. You melt it."

"Trixie's hot water could prob'ly do that, too," Bobby asserted.

Dan sat directly opposite Juliana. He reached across the table and lifted her hand, tilting the ring till the diamonds shimmered. His black eyes were unreadable when he told her, "Take very good care of this ring, Juliana." Finding himself the center of attention, he laughed nervously. "Hey! I never touched a real engagement ring before. It's kind of special, don't you agree?"

"I agree," Juliana said softly. "It's very special."

Remembering the lost, injured, and lonely girl who had come from the hospital to Crabapple Farm, Trixie's eyes dampened. How sad it would have been if she had never remembered who she was. How sad for Hans Vorwald across the sea in Amsterdam, and how sad for nameless "Janie." Yet here were the two of them, gloriously happy because the Bob-Whites had solved the mystery that turned "Janie" into Juliana again.

It mattered that Trixie and Honey made use of the

talent they had to help people with their problems. But for them, Jim Frayne might still be a hungry runaway. Yet here he sat, Honey's brother by adoption, with a fortune in trust for wise use when he was grown. And Dan might have landed in prison. Instead, he had found work and friends. Di had been letting her family's changing fortunes make her miserable and lonely. Now she was a well-loved friend, though troubled temporarily. At one time or another, each member of the Bob-Whites had faced loneliness or danger, yet here they all were, sharing this happy moment with Hans and Juliana.

Trixie had been thinking, *It matters . . .* and suddenly this became, *I matter.* Then she knew why she had flared at Hallie earlier that day. She had felt pushed aside.

Across the table, seated next to Dan, Honey sat with her face softly framed by long honey-blond hair. She looked up and smiled. Trixie wanted to tell Honey how lucky she felt to have her for a friend and how important it was to pursue a life's dream, but all she could do at the moment was to smile back.

With the Bob-Whites helping, dishes and utensils were soon cleaned and stored away. One would never have guessed that a few of the workers were used to maid service.

With the day's work done, the Beldens and their friends gathered on the wide porch to relax in the cool downdraft from the glen. At first they all chattered about the weather, the raspberries, and the

Lynch robbery. Gradually voices became silent, and Peter Belden picked up the ukulele he had kept from his own young years. While he accompanied the others, they sang the old sweet songs that fitted the mood of the evening.

Once Hans said, "I thought American music was different. More—" He chopped the air with one hand.

"Like this?" Mart clapped his hands and stamped his feet in a rock beat. His father chuckled, matching the rhythm on the ukulele while everybody clapped. With a whoop, Mart pulled Hallie to her feet. Silhouetted against the setting sun, they performed a stamping, twisting dance on the grass. Dan cut in, and Mart collapsed on the steps.

"That was very nice, Mart!" Di exclaimed, her mood obviously brightened by the wild activity.

"Nice?" Mart repeated. "Better than that, by far. Hallie excels at the terpsichorean art!"

Solemnly Bobby said, "Hallie doesn't look sick."

"Maybe it isn't catching," Hallie called over her shoulder.

Jim and Trixie joined the dance. Brian and Honey continued clapping while Peter Belden played his ukulele. Even Hans tapped his foot.

"Want to dance?" Juliana invited him.

"Are you asking me to throw my spine out of alignment?" Hans retorted. "I'll wait for a waltz."

"One waltz, coming up," Mr. Belden said. At once he switched to a Hawaiian melody that completely confused the dancers on the grass. Hans and Juliana danced alone on the porch. The others returned to the steps, with Dan making sure there was a place for Hallie to sit.

Trixie was not used to sharing the limelight, and she didn't quite know how to make room for her cousin in this fun time. She sensed that this was also true for Di and Honey.

All summer, Bobby had been trying to learn to play his father's ukulele. Mr. Belden placed the small boy's pudgy fingers on the instrument and set him to strumming.

Honey asked Bobby if he could play "Good Night, Ladies." He couldn't, but he tried mightily. Honey sang as sweetly as if he had not missed a note, then hugged him to say thank you.

When the guests had gone, Trixie went to the kitchen to set the drop-leaf table. Hallie followed. She slapped her brow when she saw Trixie's actions. "We're not eating again!"

"I'm setting the table for breakfast. I have to pick berries with the boys in the morning."

"I'll help."

Trixie stared at Hallie's long, bare legs and arms. Hallie answered the look. "I'll wear Cap's grubbies."

Trixie realized that Hallie was trying to make amends for a day gone wrong in many small ways. She appreciated the gesture and extended her own olive branch. "We better unpack them tonight. We'll get up pretty early tomorrow so we can finish our picking before it gets too hot."

The next morning, the bushes were moist with dew when Brian, Mart, Hallie, and Trixie set to work. "Just call us the 'Early Kids,'" Hallie quipped.

Mart laughed. Trixie turned to stare at this cousin who looked like a teen-age model and worked like a field hand. The fight seemed to have gone out of their relationship this morning, but Trixie wasn't in tune with Hallie's brand of humor. Not yet. Hallie herself was as warily polite with Trixie as Trixie was with her. Only with the boys was Hallie completely at ease.

Trixie sighed. If only she looked like Hallie. . . . What she wouldn't give to be long-legged, slim, and darkly beautiful!

She heard Mart grumbling about suckers sprouting several feet from the raspberry stalks. Hallie countered that the pickers might be the "suckers" for having left their beds so early. Brian's long hands moved swiftly. It was in Belden blood to love the land, but only Mart planned to make farming his life's work. He was picking berries because he enjoyed being close to the soil. Brian was there to serve the family. Trixie was there because her mother had given an order.

Why, Trixie wondered, was Hallie there? Looking like the Scarecrow from *The Wizard of Oz* in Cap Belden's camp grubbies, she worked steadily. Each time she took her rack of cartons to the cooler, Mart and Brian were right there beside her, their cartons heaped high with berries. If Trixie happened to have hers full, she went with them. If she didn't, she just enjoyed the cool morning till the three came back to the job.

A robin decided that pickings were easy in her carton, and he helped himself. She muttered, "Thief," but let him feed. Suddenly she burst out with, "Early! Kids! Those were the words on the crumpled paper in Di's fireplace!"

Brian raised his dark head to grin at her. "I wondered how long it would take you to get that."

Trixie threw a fat berry toward him. Brian caught it and stuck it in his mouth. He said, "I think we all agree that those words are a direct order from the boss man to his crew."

Trixie's sandy curls bobbed as she nodded. "Sergeant Molinson agrees, too, or he wouldn't have talked to a reporter about it. The order came from the country club. I saw the same kind of note pad by the telephone there. So the boss was an employee, or a board member, or a guest—"

"—or a tradesman, or a salesman, or a deliveryman," Mart took up the chant.

"Thieves don't have bosses. They want to do it themselves," Hallie objected.

Brian told her, "Some of them couldn't work without direction."

"You mean they're stupid," Trixie said.

"Why else would they be thieves?" Brian countered.

"Well, they did drop the wad of paper that practically left their boss's forwarding address," Trixie said. "If I were that boss, I think I'd get out of there fast." Her eyes grew round. "Maybe—he—did! Mr. Lynch said that comic with the funny name quit!"

"I'll wager—" As his round blue eyes opened wider, Mart looked so much like Trixie that both Brian and Hallie laughed. "Cease the hilarity!" he ordered. "I have a theory to propound!"

"I've pounded it first!" Trixie shouted. "That man was right there where he could get the names and addresses of all those people whose houses were crammed with stuff he could resell! I'm going to call Sergeant Molinson!" Leaving her berries, Trixie raced to the house. She returned within minutes.

"Detective Belden scored again!" Mart whooped.

"No!" Trixie snapped. "I was scooped."

"Molinson beat you to it?" Brian asked.

"It's in the morning paper. Dad was sitting on the steps reading all about it. The police are sure Oliver Tolliver was involved in the robberies, but he's disappeared. It seems he's been under suspicion for some time. He always works country clubs. He studies the members to see who looks worth robbing, then learns their names and addresses. He knows who isn't home because they're sitting right there laughing at him. While they're laughing, he catches them off guard. They let him know which house has a dog, or—"

"He overlooked Manchu—the dog in the house on Bowling Green!" Mart put in.

"We can't all be perfect," Brian said dryly.

"Anyway, that's how Sergeant Molinson sums up the boss's *modus operandi*," Trixie concluded.

Hallie sighed loudly. "Now *you're* doing it, Trixie! It'll be so good to talk with Cap when I get home. He wouldn't recognize a three-syllable word if he tripped over it."

"It would seem that our amazing mentalist had good cause to go underground," Mart declared.

"Maybe . . ." Trixie mused, feeling her excitement grow.

"Hey!" Mart objected. "No sleuthing allowed till after the wedding."

At that moment, Trixie was facing the house. She saw Bobby leave the kitchen and sidle past his father. When he reached Mrs. Belden's bed of prize dahlias, he seemed to consider himself well hidden. He pulled a package from under his shirt and headed for the gate that opened on the woods path. Almost at once, she heard a clumsy imitation of a birdcall. What kind of game was Bobby playing this morning? With Bobby, one never knew.

Before Trixie could pursue further her speculations about Oliver Tolliver, the amazing mentalist, Mrs. Belden tapped the gong that hung on the back porch. The berry pickers rinsed their hands at the garden tap and raced to the kitchen. Bobby beat them to the door and slid into his chair at the table.

Mart sniffed the air and crowed, "Did ever a mortal smell a more delectable odor than corn muffins and bacon?"

"Odor, yes, but without much substance," Mrs. Belden said. "We're short of bacon this morning. I was sure I had an extra two-pound package, but if it's in the refrigerator, I can't find it."

Mart was always hungry, and he didn't hide his disappointment. Bobby said quickly, "Mart can have my share, Moms."

"I don't believe it!" Mart said in honest astonishment. "Thanks, Bobby!"

Bobby squirmed, then busily smeared butter on a muffin.

By ten o'clock, the berries were stored in the cooler, and Mrs. Belden declared a holiday. "You've all earned it."

Freshly showered, Trixie called Honey, who told her, "We have to exercise the horses." Trixie promised help at once.

Usually Bobby howled to be included, but not today. "What's on your agenda?" Brian asked him.

Bobby was doubtful. "I don't know if I have a gender."

"An outline. A plan."

"Oh." Bobby put on his angel face. "Maybe I got a club meeting. Maybe." He seemed to argue with himself and win. "Anyway, it's 'portant."

Brian hugged Bobby's sturdy shoulders. "Being important—that's important!" But Bobby thought it was hard.

"What's so hard about playing in the woods?" Trixie asked. Bobby turned abruptly and left the room as a puzzled Trixie stared after him.

When the Beldens reached the stable, Trixie called, "Where are Honey and Jim?"

Regan, the red-haired groom, motioned toward the inside of the stables, then went back to stacking baled straw in the wide dirt-floored alleyway. Honey called from the tack room, "Here!"

Hallie stopped in the doorway. She looked at the concrete-floored tack room with its cabinets and workbenches. Saddles and bridles were racked on two walls, and blankets were neatly folded on a wide shelf. Having greeted Honey and Jim, she took a second slow look around the room. "Anything we use has to be cleaned up and put back where it belongs, right?"

"Right," said Trixie as she reached for Susie's saddle.

"Well, what's wrong with riding bareback?" Hallie demanded. "We wouldn't have to mess around cleaning tack, and we'd have more time for just plain fun."

Giggling, Honey agreed.

"Hold it!" Regan called. "I heard that! The Turf Show—"

"I know, I know, Regan," Honey called back. "But who needs the exercise? Horses or riders?"

Regan stamped down the alleyway. "Both!"

"Just this once, please, Regan?" Honey coaxed. "These kids have been picking raspberries all morning. They could use some fun. So could Jim and I."

"All right," Regan agreed. "I give up. Bareback it is. At least it'll give the horses a chance to associate with riders."

In the happy confusion of bridling the sleek animals, Regan came forward to meet Hallie. Regan was a friend and confidant of long standing, totally in charge of the stable all the time and of young people when they stepped into his domain. Suddenly Trixie realized it was important that Regan like Hallie. Did he?

Hallie grinned at Regan and said, "Howdy."

Regan grinned back, and Trixie relaxed. Hallie had not added "pard" to her "howdy." She had definitely passed the test.

Ashes From a Bonfire • 7

WHEN THE RIDERS reached Mr. Maypenny's cottage, Dan greeted them and quickly got Spartan bridled. Hallie had been happy to ride double with Mart on Strawberry, but she willingly changed horses, if not in the middle of a stream, at least in the middle of a path. With her long arms barely touching Dan's waist for balance, Hallie rode easily.

The group formed a line, with Dan and Hallie ahead of Jim, who was on Jupiter, followed by Trixie on Susie and Honey on Lady. Dan said he had been riding Manor House land all day.

"Why do you call your home Manor House?" Hallie asked Jim.

"Because these cloves and kills were first settled by the Dutch," he began.

"Cloves and kills?" Hallie repeated.

"The gullies are cloves, and the streams are kills," Jim went on. "There are about forty kills in the Catskills. See? That's part of the name. The Dutch West India Company parceled out land, especially on the east bank of the Hudson. Those parcels were called patroonships, or manors. Our land, for instance, has been cultivated since 1700. Colonial settlers, Indians, Revolutionary patriots, British soldiers, slaves, wild animals, and ghosts have all walked here."

"Wow!" Hallie exclaimed. "That makes Idaho a Johnny-come-lately." Then she added more softly, "Like me."

Totally relaxed, Trixie listened to the conversation and enjoyed the ride. Suddenly she shook herself awake. Something was different, but what was it?

A quick glance told her that nothing about the riders and their mounts had changed. It had to be something in the scene itself. She looked at leaf mold, evergreen needles, old cones, wild shrubbery, and the healthy boles of a variety of trees—fir, spruce, and white pine. With the stirring of a faint breeze came an odor she recognized—damp ashes. Someone had doused a fire recently.

"Have we had poachers?" she asked.

No one answered.

"A trespasser?" Trixie persisted.

"Not that I know of," Jim finally replied. He looked

at Dan, whose job it was to ride these forest trails. Dan wore the boxed-in expression he had brought from the streets of New York. If Dan knew anything, he was keeping it to himself.

"We can't afford a forest fire," Trixie warned. "Besides the game preserve, there are a lot of homes that would burn if a fire spread. Ours would!"

"I thought of that!" Dan flared. He made himself calm down, but his dark face remained flushed. "I thought of a lot of things. Don't worry, Trix. I put out the fire myself. Taking care of—things—is my job, you know."

Hans and Juliana were just coming back from a long walk when the riders returned to the stable. Juliana made a fist with her left hand and waggled her wrist at Dan. "See? I haven't lost my ring yet, Dan."

"Be sure that you don't," he told her. "See you later."

Back at Crabapple Farm, after the kitchen work in preparation for dinner was done, Trixie went to her room. Hallie followed but didn't enter until Trixie asked her in.

Nothing had been said about wheelchairs since the blowup in the parking lot. Still, the puzzle of Bobby's story remained. Standing at the window overlooking the lane, Trixie muttered, "There has to be an explanation, and I'm going to find it."

Hallie left the room and came back with Cap's binoculars. She gave them to Trixie. Frustrated, Trixie complained, "I can't see a thing with these that

I can't see with my own two eyes. The only difference is that I can see everything more clearly." Hallie was prowling the room. "If you have something to say, say it!" Trixie demanded.

"Bobby didn't say he stayed at that window."

"No . . . he didn't," Trixie agreed.

"Well?"

Trixie ran to the window by her desk. "With our house sitting down here in a bowl, we get a worm's-eye view of Glen Road." She was silent while she looked, then said, "There. I do see a mailbox, but I don't know whose it is. I see it through the trees." She ran to the hall and reached for the telephone.

"Who are you calling?" Hallie asked.

"Jim," Trixie said. When she heard his voice on the line, Trixie immediately asked, "Will you do something for me, Jim?"

"Silly question," Hallie whispered.

"Jim, will you drive down Glen Road, almost to town, then turn around and come back here? And each time you pass a mailbox, will you look at your watch and write down the time? There are such a few that it won't take long. Let's synchronize your watch and my desk clock. Okay?"

When Jim agreed, Trixie hung up. She told Hallie, "Once and for all, we'll know where Bobby saw that wheelchair." Until Hallie smiled, Trixie didn't realize that she'd said "we." She blushed self-consciously but allowed the word to stand. She was beginning to include Hallie Belden.

Trixie stood at the window, and Hallie faced the clock, armed with pencil and note pad. While they gave Jim time to reach the mailbox, they talked about their horseback ride.

"I couldn't keep track of where we rode," Hallie commented. "I'd hate to get lost in those woods."

Trixie nodded. "Up where those firs grow, it's pretty high and rugged. If there'd been a straight trail, we could have ridden to the stable behind the Manor House in just a few minutes. There is a footpath through that part of the woods. Sometimes we ride bicycles on it down the hill from the stable. Except for crossing Glen Road, the path's all on private land. In fact, it goes all the way to the inn."

Trixie snapped to attention. "I see Jim's car, and now—he's going in front of that mailbox. What time is it?"

"It's exactly four thirty-five," Hallie answered as she wrote it down.

The girls waited for Jim in the yard. Before he came to a full stop, he called, "I can't stay. Mother says we have to be on time for dinner. Juliana's making something special to prove to Hans that she can cook."

Trixie interrupted. "Where were you at four thirty-five?"

"In front of Di's mailbox. Why?"

"That's when we saw you with the binoculars."

"Well, that's where the action is," Hallie said. "Bobby must have seen Di's invitation being stolen. But why would anyone steal an invitation?"

"Because he was lonesome?" Jim teased.

"Curiosity?" Trixie offered.

"Information," Jim said, turning sober. "When you think of it, there's quite a lot of information on a wedding invitation—the place, the date, and the exact time when a lot of people will be sitting in one spot together. It tells who's involved and why. It gives the exact names of two generations of people."

Round-eyed, Trixie declared, "You'd make a good crook, Jim Frayne! That's exactly how Oliver Tolliver, the mentalist, operates in the country clubs. Do you suppose he stole the wheelchair and the invitation before he disappeared?"

"But why would he want the wheelchair?" Hallie asked.

"If we knew that, there wouldn't be any mystery," Trixie said, stirred with inner excitement. That something unusual was going on, she had no doubt.

After Jim had gone home, Trixie said, "That comic's disappeared. But—if we can find that wheelchair, maybe it'll lead to him."

"*If* he stole it," Hallie added.

Trixie snapped her fingers. "The hospital supply company! Remember? Hattie mentioned it."

"It's almost closing time in an office," Hallie said.

At the telephone, Trixie handed the directory to Hallie. "Read the number for me. I haven't time to waste dialing the wrong one."

Almost at once, a voice answered, "White Plains Hospital Supply. May I help you?"

"I'm calling about the wheelchair that disappeared on Glen Road." Trixie crossed her fingers.

"Miss Parker will speak to you. One moment."

When Miss Parker answered, Trixie repeated her words. "Oh, yes," said Miss Parker. "There was a mistake about the delivery address. I'm sorry. Is there some change about your present order to deliver the chair to Glen Road Inn?"

Trixie gulped. She stammered, "I—I—"

Miss Parker misinterpreted Trixie's hesitation. "Room two-fourteen. Right?"

Feeling somewhat dishonest, but glad to have the information, Trixie said, "Right. Thank you."

"I'm sorry you've been inconvenienced. You'll have the chair by eight tonight, as ordered. I have confirmation from Teed Moving Service. They now have the chair."

The instant Trixie replaced the phone, Hallie demanded, "Tell me!" When Trixie had reported all of Miss Parker's comments, Hallie said, "So that chair goes where it was supposed to go in the first place. Big deal. What can that prove?"

"I won't know unless I go to the inn to see who gets the chair!"

"So it's a little old lady in tennis shoes. Then what?"

"Then we look around to see if that man we saw pushing the wheelchair shows up," Trixie said obstinately, her stubborn streak showing.

Admiration shone in Hallie's berry-black eyes. "You don't give up, do you?"

"No. Not when someone spills a puzzle and loses a piece."

Trixie picked up the phone again and dialed the Wheelers' number. She reached Honey in her room, dressing for dinner. "Honey, please, will you bike with me tonight?"

"Isn't it pretty warm? Wouldn't you rather swim?"

"We can do both," Trixie pleaded. "It's important, Honey. You won't have to ride back up the hill to your house. Brian will be glad—"

Brian came through the hallway. "What will I be so glad to do?"

"Drive us to the lake for a swim," Trixie told him. When he nodded his assent, she continued talking to Honey. "Brian says yes. I'll see you. Is seven-thirty at the mailbox okay?"

Hallie was playing jacks with Bobby when Trixie went to meet Honey. She didn't indicate that she felt left out, and Trixie didn't invite her to go along. It would be good to spend some time alone with Honey. Not even Di was included in everything that Trixie and Honey did.

As the two girls rode slowly down Glen Road, Trixie reported her call to the hospital supply company. Jim had already told Honey about having checked the mailboxes. Like Hallie, Honey thought the delivery of the wheelchair to Glen Road Inn should end the matter. "Now we can get on with the wedding preparations," Honey coaxed.

"Maybe not," Trixie said stubbornly. "Did Di get

an invitation? She's never mentioned it again."

"Yes, she did. Miss Trask made a special trip up to the Lynch house and delivered it in person." Honey wobbled to a stop and asked Trixie, "What's that room number at the inn?"

"Two-fourteen."

"Well, no wonder there was a delivery mix-up. That's the mailbox number at the Frayne property."

"I didn't think of that," Trixie said. "Two-fourteen Glen Road. Room two-fourteen, Glen Road Inn. Even a good secretary could make that mistake."

Glen Road Inn was a large brick house, very old and of Dutch design. It had been one of the original manor houses of the area. Once frequented by the wealthy, it was now mainly a tourist stopover. Most of the rooms overlooked gardens.

The girls stopped at the desk for directions to room 214. The desk clerk was working a crossword puzzle. He pointed the way to the room, then went back to his puzzle.

As she followed Trixie down the hall, Honey whispered, "What are we going to say? We ought to have some plan before we knock on the door."

"I'll think of something," Trixie promised.

As it happened, Trixie wasn't forced to invent a reason for calling. No one answered the door. Trixie and Honey walked back to the desk. Business was slow, and having solved his puzzle, the desk clerk had plenty of time to talk. "How was Miss Ryks?"

"She wasn't," Trixie replied in a frustrated tone of

voice. "She didn't answer her door."

After a bike ride on the twenty-first of July, it was easy to look tired enough to be invited to rest in the lobby, and Trixie and Honey managed it. They sat side by side on chairs near the desk and waited for the Teed deliveryman.

"What do you expect to find out, Trixie?" Honey whispered.

"I don't know," Trixie said softly. "It just seems to me that this is our last chance to check on that wheelchair before it drops out of sight like that Oliver Tolliver. There's something fishy about an empty wheelchair and a stolen wedding invitation. I have a funny feeling!"

Honey knew about Trixie's feelings and respected them. They weren't strange intuitions or wild hunches. Trixie was a down-to-earth person, keenly aware of information gathered by all of her five senses—plus that extra sense called horse sense. When Trixie had a feeling, it meant that her brain hadn't finished running all the information through its mental computer.

Honey rubbed the carpet with one foot. She tried to think of some plausible reason why a stranger would take a wedding invitation from a mailbox and push an empty wheelchair down Glen Road on a hot July afternoon. Trixie was right. There was something fishy about the combination.

Suddenly Honey clutched Trixie's arm. "Miss Ryks!"

"Who? Where?" Trixie stared about the lobby.

"The name!" Honey said excitedly. "Miss Ryks! That's the person who called Hans and asked to be included on the guest list. Remember?"

"You're right," Trixie gasped. "Her wheelchair's missing—and she needs a wedding invitation." That was too much of a coincidence for Trixie, and she said so.

Honey argued, "We've worked together long enough to know coincidence plays a big part in solving a mystery, Trixie Belden."

"Gleeps, Honey! Coincidence usually takes us down a dead-end street." Trixie's attention bounced in another direction. "Wasn't Miss Trask to call Miss Ryks? What did she find out? Is Miss Ryks a friend of the Maasdens or the Vorwalds?"

"Miss Trask tried to call her, but she wasn't in."

"Well, that solves one problem," Trixie said cheerfully. "Now we know what we can say if she does answer that door. We can say we have mutual friends —Juliana Maasden and Hans Vorwald."

"Yes-s," Honey breathed. "That'll work."

The air conditioner was on, but in the lobby, it managed only to move hot air from one place and deposit it in another. Trixie pushed her short mop of curls up from the nape of her neck and sighed. "I wish that deliveryman would come before my brains melt."

They didn't have long to wait. The man came through the door, notebook in hand. At the desk, he thumbed his visored cap back from his brow and asked, "Ya got a Miss Ryks here, room two-fourteen? Well, I got this wheelchair, see, and I don't want no mix-up. If it ain't too much bother, I'd kinda like you to witness that I delivered this pesky contraption. Okay?"

"Okay with me," the desk clerk said. "Side door."

With no loss of time, the talkative young driver appeared at the service entrance, pushing a wheel-chair. The clerk left the desk and took him down the intersecting hall to room 214. Trixie started to follow, but Honey held her back. "We can't snoop, Trixie."

"Who's snooping?" Trixie argued. "Anybody can walk down a hall! Besides, the clerk knows we tried to see Miss Ryks. Come on. We'll stay out of sight."

"We know the wheelchair is being delivered. Isn't that enough?" Honey begged.

"I want to see it with my own eyes," Trixie said with finality, and Honey gave in. Both girls stationed themselves in the service hall within sight and hear-ing of room 214.

Bare Cupboards • 8

THERE WAS A WAIT at the door of room 214. The clerk knocked several times while the driver fluttered pages of his notebook. The door was opened by a bare-foot young man wearing hiphugger jeans and a stretched-out T-shirt. Stringy brass-colored hair hung limply to the top of the neckband. An equally stringy moustache hid his mouth, and huge dark glasses hid his eyes. In a nasal voice, he said, "I'll sign. I'm Miss Ryks's nephew. Miss Ryks is sacked out. Indisposed."

He signed the receipt, accepted the wheelchair, pulled it into the room, and closed the door. Trixie and Honey ducked through the service entrance door before the Teed man turned the corner of the hall. The girls were busy unlocking their bikes when he drove away in the same pickup that Hallie had seen at Wimpy's.

"I wonder," Trixie worried, "if we should go back and try again to see Miss Ryks. If we could describe her, maybe Hans or Juliana would recognize her."

"We can't go back. She's sick."

"She can't be all that sick," Trixie argued. "She expects to be well enough in two weeks to go to a wedding, doesn't she?"

Trixie straddled her bicycle but kept both feet on the parking lot pavement. "Miss Ryks should be told about that wheelchair. If it was stolen once, it can be stolen again, and there she'd be, unable to attend the wedding of her dear old friends, and—"

Honey giggled. "Dear old friends! Trixie, neither Hans nor Juliana ever heard of her!"

"Well, she's heard of them," Trixie said. "Right now, let's get back to that wheelchair. We know a man caught a ride with the Teed driver. We've seen the truck. No chair could fall out, so somebody lifted it out. Probably the hitchhiker. He could have hidden the chair to collect the reward money. Right?"

"You saw the man pushing the chair. Did he look like a thief?" Honey asked.

"How do I know what a thief looks like? The point is, there's a man with sticky fingers who hasn't been caught yet. He's not just greedy—he's mean. He knew someone was helpless without that chair. Isn't it our civic duty to do something about people like him?"

Honey was more lenient. "Maybe he didn't give that a thought. When I have a problem, I don't always think of how my actions will affect other people."

"Oh, you!" Trixie scoffed affectionately. "You're at the head of the line when it comes to considering other people." Trixie scanned the parking lot, where the night-lights had just been turned on. She grinned at Honey. "Can you spot a wheelchair thief right this minute? Well, neither can I, so let's go home."

Honey bent to retie a shoelace before getting on her bike. While Trixie waited for her, she rode in a slow, wobbling circle, appreciating the shadows that cooled the old brick walls of the inn. She watched a well-fed cat walk toward the back of the building. Evidently it was headed for the kitchen door, where a row of garbage cans had been set out for the trash collector. Suddenly Trixie began pedaling at a furious rate after the cat.

"Trixie! Have you lost your mind?" Honey, too, joined the cat's parade.

"It's Hallie!" Trixie yelled. "I saw her leave the rear of the building."

"You must be wrong," Honey insisted.

But Trixie wasn't wrong. Hallie saw them coming and waited in the paved area near the garbage cans.

"What are you doing here, Hallie Belden?" Trixie yelled.

"Same thing you are," Hallie retorted. "Snooping."

Immediately on the defensive, Trixie said angrily,

"I'm not snooping! I'm investigating! I *knew* it would be like this. Not a minute to myself! We agreed on no kissy-kissy, but you're obviously still whacko-whacko!" Trixie took a deep breath, almost prepared to pick up her previous show of temper where she'd left off. Then she smiled instead. "I did it again, didn't I, Hallie? I'm sorry. What did you find out?"

To Trixie's surprise, tears ran down Hallie's brown face. In alarm, Trixie asked, "Is—is something wrong?" She'd never seen Hallie Belden cry.

Hallie swiped at the tears with the back of a hand. "That's the first time you ever said 'sorry' when you didn't have to," she gulped.

"Oh." Too embarrassed to continue her questioning, Trixie stared at the only object close at hand—that stray cat.

Honey rushed to Trixie's rescue. "What *did* you find out, Hallie? We know who ordered the chair."

"Miss Ryks," Hallie confirmed. "Well, I found out that she has strange eating habits. She's been here two days, but she's never been to the dining room, and she hasn't ordered a bite of food from the kitchen. Then just a few minutes ago, she ordered liver and onions."

"But that nephew said—" Trixie turned to Honey, who finished the sentence.

"—indisposed. What a peculiar diet for an invalid!" Honey's puzzled expression changed to a smile. "Okay if we go swimming now?" she pleaded. "Brian's going to have his nose glued to a medical journal if he has to wait for us much longer, and I'll have to ride all the way up that hill after all."

"If that happens, we'll run along behind and push," Trixie promised. "Let's go."

As they left the inn, Honey said, "There's a new ten-speed bike just like Jim's."

A gate stood open where a brick walk branched off from the kitchen pavement and disappeared into a shadowy curve between the building and a hedge of lilacs. Partially hidden on the walk was a bicycle. It looked so new that a price tag might have dangled from the handlebars. Just like Jim's, the bike was blue. But this one had a scratch.

As they neared the farm, Trixie asked Hallie, "How'd you happen to go to the kitchen?"

"My mother's a smart kid," Hallie drawled. "She says that if you want to get acquainted with a new neighbor, go to the back door." She slanted a glance at Trixie. "I really didn't mean to interfere. I didn't know what you had in mind, so I just thought I'd hang around in case you ran into that Oliver Tolliver and needed help. He spells trouble."

"How'd you get in, Hallie?" Honey asked.

"I said I was thirsty and asked if I could please have a drink of water. It was after the dinner hour, and the cook was griping because this order came in when she wanted to watch a TV program. She didn't want to mess around with onions."

"Well," Trixie mused, "all we know is that Miss Ryks is an oddball."

"A sick oddball," Honey corrected.

"Sick!" chorused the Belden cousins. "Eating liver and onions?"

"Anyway, she needs a wheelchair," Honey said.

At the farm, the girls found Brian sitting in the jalopy, reading a medical journal by flashlight. Bathing suits and towels were heaped in the backseat. Mart was playing tag with Bobby but vaulted into the jalopy when he saw the three girls.

Mrs. Belden called from the porch swing, "Brian, please stop at Mr. Lytell's store. He'll let you have a couple of loaves of bread if you go to the back door. I can't imagine how we ran out before baking day!"

The next morning, the shortage of food came up again. Mrs. Belden said, "I do wish you boys would check up on our chickens' diet. With both a future doctor and a future farmer in the house, we should be able to keep a few hens laying. There wasn't one egg yesterday."

While his mother was speaking, Mart slid a second egg onto his plate. He paused, server in midair. "Am I taking more than my share, Moms?"

Quickly Bobby said, "You can have mine, Mart. I'm kind of not hungry."

Mr. Belden peered over the wall of his newspaper. "What's all this sudden concern for Mart's appetite, Robert Belden?" he asked. "I'm the provider for this household. If we don't get enough eggs from our hens, we'll buy them from Mr. Lytell."

Mart thumped Bobby's back. "You shared bacon

with me. Now I'll share an egg with you. Okay?"

Bobby tried to put on his angel face but didn't quite manage it. His lips trembled. "Can I be 'scused?"

Mrs. Belden shook her head. "Peter, I'm puzzled. Maybe I'm turning into the old woman in the shoe. My cupboards are bare!"

"Wrong nursery rhyme, Moms!" Mart teased.

It was early that evening when the young people of Glen Road gathered at Crabapple Farm. The day had been hot, but a downdraft of evening coolness moved toward the Hudson through the clove where the farm lay. Each person found a comfortable lounging spot on the porch or in the yard. Hans didn't talk much, but each time he did speak up, Trixie turned to listen. She liked the sound of English words on a tongue that had spoken Dutch from babyhood. There was a trace of the same accent in Juliana's voice, but she'd learned English well enough to use American slang. It amused all of them to explain a word or phrase to Hans.

Because she was listening so intently, Trixie noticed a soft *thump, thump*. She heard a faint rumble in Reddy's throat. His head lifted, ears alert, and his feathery red tail moved nervously. Trixie slid along the porch step she shared with Di and Honey until she was next to the dog. She whispered, "What do you see, Reddy?"

"He hears something, that's for sure," Dan said.

Even though Trixie's fingers smoothed his velvet ears, Reddy didn't relax. Something hidden by the shadows was bothering him.

The talk was about the wedding. Always interested in clothes, Di asked eagerly, "What will you wear, Juliana?"

"Just a summer dress," Juliana answered. "I know Miss Trask has followed Mrs. Wheeler's instructions about sending out invitations, but neither Hans nor I want formality. We'll live in an apartment in Amsterdam, and our life will be very simple. I've been away so long that I've lost touch with old friends. Even in Amsterdam, we'd have had a plain civil ceremony."

"You must wear white," Mrs. Belden said. "Would you like to wear my wedding dress?"

"I'd love it, but I can't let you alter it," Juliana insisted. "You must save it for Trixie."

Reddy was so restless that Trixie found it hard to take part in the conversation. She noticed that Dan, too, stared into the dark each time Reddy made a sound. For some reason, Dan refused to give up his place beside Juliana, even when Bobby tried to squirm between them.

Trixie heard Hans tell Mr. Belden, "No, sir. We won't use Juliana's inheritance right away. We'll save the money to educate our children." Trixie hoped that the life of the young Vorwalds would settle into a comfortable routine. *Like our own, maybe,* she thought.

When Honey and Di married, it would be with pomp and ceremony. Family wealth demanded it.

That's not for me, Trixie thought. She would wear her mother's dress in a simple and lovely home ceremony, and that dress would probably remain in the family for generations.

"Mrs. Vanderpoel!" Trixie cried, surprising herself as much as the group. Mrs. Belden peered expectantly into the dark, and Trixie giggled. "Sit still, Moms. She isn't coming up the lane. I was thinking about wedding dresses, and I remembered Mrs. Vanderpoel's attic. I'll bet she's got every wedding dress anybody in her family ever wore. I know Juliana wants to keep things simple, but Miss Trask has invited all those people, and ordered the wedding cake, and hired an organist." Trixie spread her hands. "Miss Trask and Mrs. Wheeler are going right ahead planning a real wedding. I mean—"

"Traditional," Mart put in.

Honey fluttered her hands. "You know how Mother loves tradition, Juliana. If there's a way to find a wedding dress on such short notice, wouldn't you wear it?"

"Well. . . ."

"Mrs. Vanderpoel is about your height," Honey coaxed.

"If you say she's the same size, I'll insist that Dad send you to have your eyes examined, Honey Wheeler," Jim said.

"Three Julianas would fit inside one of Mrs. Vanderpoel's dresses," Dan scoffed.

"Don't be so sure about that, Dan," Honey said.

"Mrs. Vanderpoel was young once."

"Judging from her bone structure," doctor-to-be Brian said, "she may have been Juliana's size when she married. What do you think, Moms?"

"Let's go find out!" Trixie jumped up, ready for action. Reddy hadn't given up shadow watching. When Trixie stood, so did he, and every hair on the ridge of his spine bristled like a porcupine quill.

The Bob-Whites, plus Juliana, Hallie, and Hans, ran to the station wagon parked in the deep shadow of an ancient oak. Just for an instant, Trixie felt crowded, as if too many people were present. Then she was distracted by the sudden movement of Reddy chasing the thump of running feet.

"Don't hurry me, Hans. It's too dark to see where I'm going," Juliana said breathlessly.

"Who's hurrying you?" Hans asked.

"Aren't you?" Juliana asked. "I thought you took my hand, Hans."

"Only when you let me," Hans teased.

Jim fished a flashlight out of the glove compartment and explored the curve of the lane. Peter Belden called from the porch, "Everything all right out there?"

Jim called back, "I think so, sir."

It wasn't a long drive to Mrs. Vanderpoel's yellow brick house in the woods. Short and plump, she smiled a welcome when she opened her door. "Now, how did you know I baked windmill cookies today?"

Mart planted a kiss on the gray bun of hair on top

of her head. Mrs. Vanderpoel was his favorite neighbor. "We didn't know. We hoped."

Trixie was quite at home in this house crowded with antique furniture. Mrs. Vanderpoel lived alone but took an active part in the life of her neighborhood. She'd been involved in more than one of Trixie's mysteries and had lent her furniture for the Bob-Whites' antique show. Trixie didn't hesitate to ask her for another favor.

"Juliana had planned to be married in her best summer dress, but Miss Trask has invited so many people and made so many plans that we think Juliana should wear a real wedding dress."

Mrs. Vanderpoel's eyes twinkled. "Let me guess: You thought of my attic?"

"Right," Honey agreed with a bright smile for this good friend.

Mrs. Vanderpoel fluttered dimpled hands toward Hallie. Trixie said quickly, "My cousin Hallie."

"You're Harold's daughter! I should have recognized those long bones. You look like your father did when he was a teen-ager," Mrs. Vanderpoel said. "Now, my attic."

"If you don't mind, Mrs. Vanderpoel," Brian said, "we fellows will show Hans your house."

"Make yourselves at home."

On the way up the stairs, Juliana explained, "Our wedding is being quickly arranged. As you know, Hans came in search for me while my memory was lost. His time off from work is almost used up. Any wedding plan must be kept very simple."

"I do wish you well, child," Mrs. Vanderpoel said sincerely. She ushered the five girls into an attic that was as neat as most people's living rooms, then led them to a huge cedar chest. When she lifted the chest lid, the smells of cedar and lavender tickled their noses.

For Trixie, the next hour was one of sheer delight. She was no fashion fanatic, but she loved beautiful fabrics. These dresses, folded away in tissue paper, were proof that women had lived and loved. Their lives were woven into the very fabric of the Hudson River valley. With Trixie, the rest of the girls exclaimed over silks, satins, taffetas, and laces. They measured dress after dress against Juliana's tiny frame. The verdict was always the same—too big.

While Juliana watched, Trixie, Honey, Di, and Hallie sashayed about in dresses, swished skirts, and dreamed dreams. Finally they rewrapped the gowns and repacked the chest.

"I'm sorry, Juliana," Trixie said. "I was sure—"

"Don't give up so easily," Mrs. Vanderpoel advised. "You haven't seen my own wedding dress."

She opened a small trunk and drew out still another tissue-wrapped package. When she shook out folds of sheer white cotton, Trixie knew the search was ended. *This* was Juliana's wedding dress.

Almost shyly, Trixie took the dress from Mrs. Vanderpoel's hands and held it up by the shoulder seams. As if she were putting a dress on a paper doll, Trixie held it up against Juliana's body. Of simple design, the handmade dress was trimmed with rows and rows of crocheted insertions in the sleeves and the skirt.

"It won't have to be altered one stitch. It could have been made for you, Juliana," Honey said softly.

"I was married during the First World War," Mrs. Vanderpoel explained. "I made my own dress while I waited for my soldier to come home from France."

"Even the lace?" Trixie asked, greatly impressed.

"Every stitch." Mrs. Vanderpoel unwrapped a wide-brimmed white leghorn hat wreathed with daisies. "I was married in the garden behind this house."

Trixie clasped her hands under her chin. "The garden at Manor House is so lovely. I can just see Juliana walking past all those flowers at the birdbath. We could all wear dresses like this—" She stopped abruptly. "Where would we find them?"

Honey was practical. "We'd make them, of course."

"A garden wedding," Juliana whispered. "I know Hans will agree to that!"

The Ring · 9

Trixie was having sudden second thoughts about her own agreement with this idea—she hated to sew. She asked Honey, "What do you mean, make them?"

Honey spread the skirt of the white dress. "This isn't as hard to do as it looks. The skirt is just a long wide strip sewed onto a band. The top is a simple bodice with long sleeves and a throatband instead of a collar. It's the lace that makes it special. We needn't use as much of that, and we'd certainly buy factory-made lace. We don't want to outshine the bride."

"As if anyone could!" Di said.

Honey's blue eyes sparkled with interest. "We could use strips of lace for throatbands and put lace from the shoulder to the cuff of each sleeve."

"That sounds hard," Trixie declared.

"It isn't!" Hallie contradicted her. "Didn't you ever make doll clothes, Trixie? You just split the sleeve, insert lace the length of the sleeve, and sew it back together."

"You don't sew, Hallie Belden!" Trixie scoffed.

"Oh, don't I!" Hallie said. "Wait till I open my suitcase, and I'll show you. I made every stitch I brought with me."

"That you *didn't* bring with you!" Trixie corrected.

Honey remembered the week's previous arguments and pretended not to hear the irritation in Trixie's voice. "We won't have to worry about what's easy and what's hard. Miss Trask will call a fitter to help us."

Trixie sighed with relief. "I wouldn't be caught dead in anything I made."

"Neither would anyone else," Di giggled.

"Ribbon sashes," Honey planned, "with big flat bows, the ends of the ribbon touching the floor, and matching ribbons on our hats, and—"

"—and daisies," Di added.

"White gloves," Mrs. Vanderpoel said, "and white slippers. And even white stockings."

"Oh, yes," Juliana agreed happily. "Let's go tell Hans about our new plans."

Five excited girls went down the two flights of stairs to Mrs. Vanderpoel's living room. Trixie ran ahead with the cry, "We found it!" and Juliana danced into the room, waving her hands.

Trixie had grown used to the flash of Juliana's engagement ring, and now she missed it. "Juliana, let me see your hand."

Juliana held out both her hands and cried in dismay, "My ring! It's gone!"

Her cry caught everyone's attention immediately: "No!" "It can't be!" "Maybe it's snagged on your skirt."

Juliana stood in the middle of the room and allowed a careful search of her clothing. Hans thought she should undress in Mrs. Vanderpoel's bedroom, in case the ring had slipped inside her clothes while trying on the gowns.

"No," Juliana said worriedly, "I didn't try on the dresses. They were too large, all but one. Oh, Hans, what am I to do? Your lovely ring!" She cried, and Hans comforted her.

Hans suggested an inspection of the floors and stairs. Mrs. Vanderpoel handed out flashlights and turned on every lamp from the front door to the attic. Inch by inch, Juliana's route through the house was retraced, but the ring was not to be found.

"It may have caught on the material of one of the dresses," Mrs. Vanderpoel said.

In the attic, the sober group sat in a circle. Each person took a tissue-wrapped package, made a thorough examination of the material inside, and handed it back to Mrs. Vanderpoel. "No ring," Mart said, dismally echoing the verdict of the others.

Although they knew there was little chance for success, they searched the porch, the walk, and finally the station wagon itself. Not a flash of gold or diamonds did anyone see. Juliana cried inconsolably, distressing Hans. "You'll make yourself sick, Juliana. I'll buy another ring—one that fits."

"But it won't be the same. This was your family's heirloom ring!"

"You'll get it back," Dan said earnestly.

"How can you be so sure?" Trixie wondered.

Mrs. Vanderpoel offered to serve cookies and milk, but not even Mart was interested in food. It was a silent group that left the yellow brick house. Juliana didn't even remember to take the wedding dress and the daisy-wreathed hat.

Back at Crabapple Farm, Trixie didn't go to bed until her brothers came in from the barn. They'd helped Dan saddle Spartan for his ride back to Mr. Maypenny's cottage. Trixie could hear Dan whistling in the dark, and the sound was so sad that it made her feel lonesome. The evening had begun with gaiety, but it had ended with gloom.

Her blue mood lingered in her dreams. She was surprised that Honey could make a cheerful call early Friday morning. The Beldens were at breakfast, so Trixie took the call at her mother's kitchen desk.

"Miss Trask is all in a dither about wedding plans," Honey said. "She's already sent Jim to Mrs. Vanderpoel's to pick up the dress and hat. She's making lists of the materials needed for our outfits, and she wants to take our measurements. Di's riding over in a little while. Can your mother spare you and Hallie?"

Trixie obtained Mrs. Belden's permission, but Hallie insisted, "I'm going to stay on the phone today till I convince Cap Belden that I need my clothes! Just because he doesn't care if he ever sees his grubbies again, he thinks there's no reason why I should want my suitcase either!"

When Trixie had relayed the information to Honey and hung up, Hallie placed her call to Idaho. "Knut!" she cried. Without bothering to cover the mouthpiece, Hallie announced to the breakfasting Beldens, "He's the one with sense. Now I'll get action." Over the top of his newspaper, Peter Belden grinned at his wife.

Mart declaimed pompously, "I detect in my sire's surreptitious glance an acknowledgment that second sons of Belden clans are notably lax in the application of velocity to tasks at hand. Now, let me say in defense of my kinsman Cap, who, like me, has an elder sibling of irreproachable behavior, that undoubtedly he must make a superhuman effort to assert himself as a distinct and separate personality. That—"

"Cap's personality stinks, all right!" said Hallie inelegantly as she put down the phone. "He went to the lake and left my bag sitting right there in the hall. Knut says he'll put it on the next flight out, and when Knut makes a promise, he keeps his word!"

Hallie's black eyes flashed with such fire that Mart put up a hand to shield his face. Brian stiffened his spine and adjusted an imaginary halo. Trixie, who had awaked thinking she might never smile again, couldn't stop herself from giggling.

At Manor House, Trixie and Hallie found Miss Trask in the sewing room, measuring Honey and Di. Armed with a notebook and a tape measure, she cornered the Belden girls.

Hallie backed away. "Don't bother with me, Miss Trask. I'm not in the wedding."

"Of course you'll dress to match the other girls," Miss Trask said briskly. "Now, come here and let me measure you."

"Yes, ma'am," Hallie said meekly.

Juliana came in while Miss Trask was figuring the yardage of sheer white voile and wide satin ribbon needed. The Dutch girl's eyes showed that she had been crying, but her welcoming smile was genuine. Trixie wondered if she herself would be as brave in a similar situation.

"What color do you want, Trixie?"

Flushing with confusion, Trixie focused her blue eyes on Juliana's face. "Excuse me?"

"Choose," Juliana invited.

"Ribbon color," Honey explained.

"Blue," Trixie managed to say, knowing blue was her best color for anything from ribbons to bathing suits. She had been so concerned about Juliana's tears that she had completely lost track of the sewing room conversation.

Honey chose gold, and Diana wanted lilac. "To match my eyes," Di said, preening just a little.

"Guess that leaves pink for me," Hallie said. "I can't

119

have red?" She glanced at Miss Trask.

"No, you can't have red," Miss Trask declared.

Hallie grinned. "Just testing."

Miss Trask bustled about the room gathering up the lists she'd made. "Honey, will you please call Tom to bring around the car? I'll get my hat and bag and meet him in the porte cochere." She turned at the door to announce, "I'll leave word in the kitchen that there'll be guests for lunch. You'll stay, all of you?"

Putting the previous night's worry out of their minds, Honey, Di, Trixie, and Hallie darted down the stairs and out the side entrance to the garden, where the ancient birdbath stood.

Honey reached for Trixie's hand. "Can't you just see it? We'll arrange the chairs in rows on the grass. Hans and Jim will walk from the summerhouse with the pastor. The light will be on their faces in the late afternoon."

"Half after four o'clock," Trixie said dreamily.

"And over there," Honey went on, pointing toward a great mass of daisies, asters, pinks, and gladioli, "Juliana will walk down that winding stone path."

Starry-eyed, Di asked, "Where will we be?"

Hallie flung both hands above her head. "Oh, we'll be there, too, but the ones who matter are Hans and Juliana."

Carried away by the romance of the picture she could see, Di cried, "Let's give a shower for her!"

"Let's!" chorused the rest of the girls.

"We'll have the shower at the farm," Trixie volunteered. "Moms will love it." She saw Spartan in the alleyway near Jupiter's stall and knew Dan was on an errand. She hurried down the path to the clubhouse, shouting over her shoulder, "Dan's at the stable. Let's ride home with him. We can plan the details of the shower later."

Regan wouldn't allow another bareback ride, even when Hallie coaxed. Hallie's grin wrinkled her flat cheeks. "Well, I can *try* to get out of saddling a horse, can't I? I'm more at home on a motorbike!"

"Let me help you," Dan offered.

"And don't worry about cleaning tack when you get back," Regan added. "I'll see that Strawberry's taken care of."

"*I'm* riding Strawberry today," Di stated positively.

"That leaves Starlight for you," Regan told Hallie. "Are you sure you can manage?"

Trixie doubted that her cousin could handle Starlight. Generously she told Hallie, "You take Susie, and I'll ride Starlight." Pertly she informed Regan, "And I'll clean her tack, too."

"See that you do, missy," Regan retorted.

"That was nice of you, Trixie," Honey said warmly.

"Why not?" Trixie returned. "She's my relative."

The girls enjoyed their ride to Mr. Maypenny's cottage. The old gamekeeper had been told about the lost ring and asked if it had been found.

"No, not yet," Dan said firmly.

The girls kept careful track of the time to be sure that they'd be home when Miss Trask returned from her shopping expedition. As they were leaving, Mr. Maypenny asked Dan, "Did Regan send an answer to my note?"

Dan put a hand in his pocket. He looked worried. "I must have left my wallet at the stable. I'll ride up for it later."

"Don't bother," Honey told Dan. "Trixie and I will be glad to bring it back to you."

"Thanks."

Unused to Hallie's hands, Susie was becoming skittish. Dan spoke soothingly to the small black mare and smoothed a flank with a gentle hand. He stepped off the trail to allow the others to fall in line. He waved as they left the clearing but he didn't smile at them. Dan hadn't smiled much at anything lately.

"Dan's an okay kid," Hallie declared. Trixie agreed.

At the Manor House stable, Hallie asked, "This beast doesn't bite, does she? Looks like I'm stuck with unsaddling her after all. I'll stay close to Di and do what she does."

Trixie grinned and went with Honey to find Regan.

"Dan must have left his wallet on my desk," Regan told them. "He was messing around there when Tom asked him to give a hand with Jupiter." Regan went to the ancient rolltop desk in the corner of the tack room and raised the lid.

"Yep, here it is. Give me a minute while I write a note to Mr. Maypenny, will you?" Regan reached into a slot for paper but pulled out a folded handkerchief instead. "Now, how'd that get in there?"

Regan was a careful housekeeper. In his stable, all must be in order, even notepaper.

"That's Dan's handkerchief," Honey said. "I embroidered those initials when I gave him a set of handkerchiefs for his birthday."

Regan thrust it forward. "Take it back to him and tell him to put it in his pocket, where it belongs, and not in my—" Regan's words ran down. Slowly he unfolded the linen square. "There's something here."

Trixie caught the glint of tiny rainbows. Then Regan exposed a golden tulip whose fluted throat was filled with diamonds!

Honey clasped hands under her chin and squealed, "Juliana's ring!" Trixie stared silently at her, and Honey finished slowly, "But—D-Dan said—"

Trixie swallowed hard. "I know. We heard him tell Mr. Maypenny that the ring hadn't been found yet."

"Yet?" Regan repeated. In the cup of his hand, the diamonds glinted like accusing eyes.

"When he found it, why didn't he tell us?" Honey asked. "He knows how upset Juliana is. He knows we're all worried."

For a long moment, the three stared at the ring. Then Regan pushed it down on the tip of the little finger of his right hand. Anxiously Honey asked, "What are you going to do?"

"I must give this ring to your mother, so she can return it to Juliana," Regan said.

"Regan, you can't do that till we've talked to Dan," Trixie argued. "Just because he—he—" Trixie couldn't say "lied," since she had no clue as to how that ring got into Dan Mangan's handkerchief. Instead she pleaded, "Dan's your nephew, Regan. You have to wait and hear his side of the story."

"I'll return the ring, then talk to Dan," Regan decided. He strode up the graveled path that led to the house.

"Regan, please!" Trixie begged.

Honey put a hand on Trixie's arm to keep her from following. "It'll be all right, Trixie. Miss Trask'll take care of it." Together, Miss Trask and Regan managed the estate, even to the point of advising or disciplining the young people when necessary. They were respected and trusted by family, friends, and employees.

"Miss Trask isn't home," Trixie reminded Honey. "Regan said he's going to your mother."

"Oh."

The girls gaped at each other while possible consequences of Regan's conversation with Mrs. Wheeler flashed through their minds.

"I could bite my tongue off for what I said," Trixie lamented. "Now it sounds like Dan lied to Mr. Maypenny within our hearing, and that makes it sound like he lied to us. If he did lie, it means that he knew the ring was in his handkerchief, and if he knew it and didn't say so, then it looks like he—"

"No!" Honey said positively. "Dan wouldn't steal." She gulped. "Trixie, a Bob-White of the Glen is in trouble." She didn't have to add that this particular Bob-White had been in lots of trouble not long ago and had been put under his uncle's supervision to re-habilitate himself. Because of Dan's past, it was easy to let the blame fall on his shoulders when something went wrong—something serious like a missing diamond ring wrapped in his handkerchief.

With nothing but blind loyalty to go on, Trixie said, "Okay, Dan didn't steal that ring."

Tears rolled down Honey's cheeks. "I agree. But how are we going to prove it?"

"We will," Trixie said firmly.

Dan's whole life might be altered when Regan placed that ring in Mrs. Wheeler's hand. The society woman wasn't used to accepting personal responsibility, even for her own children. Her usual answer to all questions was, "Ask Miss Trask." At the end of the path, Regan had disappeared into the house through the servants' entrance. Right this minute, Dan's reputation was being put on a seesaw. Was Mrs. Wheeler telling Regan, "Ask Miss Trask"? Or was she calling the police?

"Mother likes Dan," Honey whispered.

Trixie added, "So does Regan."

"But—" Honey let that one word drift like a feather in the wind.

"Dan has a right to be heard," Trixie declared, and having made up her mind to take some action, she hurried to mount Starlight.

The horse and rider left the stable at a brisk trot, and Honey followed on Lady. As the girls approached the cottage in the woods, they could smell onions.

Mr. Maypenny was making lunch. He came to the door wiping his hands on a towel.

"Dan? No, he isn't here. Fact is, I thought he was up at the stable. He lit out of here so fast that I just figured he'd forgotten something and was going to catch up with you to take care of it."

Trixie listened to his cheerful speech. She couldn't tell Mr. Maypenny about the ring. However the matter turned out, it would be better if he heard the story from Dan. "Is Dan riding Spartan?" she asked the gamekeeper.

"No. That's the odd part of it. He's afoot."

"We brought Dan's wallet with your note," Honey said.

As they left the clearing, both girls waved and tried to smile. "Shall we look for Dan or go back to Manor House?" Trixie asked.

Honey waved a hand at the forest, where trees marched endlessly toward an unseen horizon. "Where would we look? Let's go see what happened at home."

Trixie nodded.

Regan met the girls at the stable and guessed where they'd been. While he helped cool their mounts, he asked, "Did you talk to Dan?" When Trixie explained that Dan wasn't at the cottage and that Mr. Maypenny didn't know where he was, Regan scowled. He said bleakly, "When I came outside, I saw Dan here, but he didn't seem to notice me. He ran."

"R-Ran?" Honey's lips quivered. "No!"

Staunchly Trixie insisted, "I'm sure that he was

126

looking for his wallet. That's all."

"That's what I figured," Regan agreed.

"To give Juliana the ring, too," Trixie went on stubbornly.

"Well—I don't know about that," Regan said. "I've seen him hanging around lately with a couple of toughs from his old street gang. Once when I asked him about it, he clammed up."

Hotly Trixie said, "You know he didn't steal that ring! You know there has to be some explanation."

"I don't know a thing until I talk to Dan," Regan said. He turned away with such an air of finality that Trixie and Honey could do nothing but stare at each other helplessly.

The Footprint • 10

Silently, the two girls left the stable and returned to the house. At last Trixie exploded. "Sometimes I wish Regan wasn't so pigheadedly loyal to the Wheelers!" She was concentrating so much on Dan's predicament at the moment that she forgot that Honey was a Wheeler.

Sounding like a lost child, Honey said, "Me, too."

Trixie turned to hug her friend. "Oh, I didn't mean you, Honey. I just meant—oh, I don't know what I meant! Of course I want Regan to be loyal."

Luncheon that day was one of the few uncomfortable meals Trixie had ever eaten at Manor House. Juliana was jubilant about the return of her ring. She flashed it in the face of each person she met and cried, "Isn't it beautiful! Oh, isn't it beautiful!"

Hans hovered close to her. He reassured each guest, "I'll have the ring made smaller, I promise!"

"What happened?" Trixie whispered to Honey. "Do you think Miss Trask knows?"

"No," Honey answered. "I saw Juliana show Miss Trask her ring. She would never have done that if Miss Trask had given it to her."

"Your mother must have delivered it to her personally," Trixie said. "Do you think she called you-know-who?"

"You know my mother," Honey said with a sigh. She called down the table, "Miss Trask, is Mother having lunch in her room?"

Jim answered the question, with a little nod of apology to Miss Trask for his interruption. "Mother got a phone call from Dad. She's having lunch with him in White Plains, and then they may go on to New York tonight. In fact, they may be gone several days."

Honey and Trixie looked blankly at each other. Where did that leave Dan?

Celia was serving. She came to the table to tell Hallie that she had a telephone call.

"Knut!" Hallie exclaimed. But when she came back to the table, she announced, "It wasn't my brother after all. The call was from Auntie, and she says my bag has arrived at the airport."

"I'll pick it up," Jim offered. "Any tagalongs?"

129

Each girl at the table cried, "Yes!"

Miss Trask asked Di and Honey if they'd mind staying behind. "I need some help to get these dresses started."

"I'll help the minute I get back," Hallie promised.

Quite pointedly, no one asked Trixie to help with the sewing. Jim commented on it and then looked puzzled when Trixie didn't respond.

On the drive to the airport, Trixie reported the latest part of the story of the missing ring. Jim scowled as he listened. "You don't suspect Dan, do you, Trix?"

"Of course not," she said. "But—" The word hung in the air till it seemed to echo inside her skull.

"I see what you mean," Jim admitted reluctantly. "Dan was there. He had the opportunity to get hold of that ring, even if only to pick it up when it slid off Juliana's finger. I wish he hadn't said 'not yet.' "

"And I wish those creeps from the city weren't hanging around again," Trixie said bitterly.

"It'll take a miracle to help him if Mother called the sergeant and Dan ran away," Jim said.

"Not a miracle," Trixie said, "but Reddy maybe."

"Reddy!" Jim exclaimed.

"You mean your dog?" Hallie asked.

"Reddy. Our dog," Trixie said. "Remember when we were getting into the wagon last night and we heard Reddy chase something into the bushes?"

"It could have been a cat or a stray calf," Jim said.

"But I felt crowded," Trixie said. "I know in my

very bones that there were too many people out there under the oak tree. Remember when Juliana said Hans was rushing her when she couldn't see and he said that he hadn't taken her hand? Well, nobody else confessed to touching her." Trixie fell silent for a moment, then voiced another thought. "Oh. Dan was there, too. I almost forgot. Just because he didn't confess doesn't mean that he didn't grab her hand and slide off the ring."

They were almost at the airport parking lot when Trixie said, "Jim, on our way back, will you drop me off about halfway up our lane?"

"Whatever for?" Hallie blurted. "I promised to help Miss Trask."

"You help me," Trixie bargained, "and I'll help you."

Jim grinned. "Okay. I'll help both of you."

There was a between-flights lull at the airport. A number of people checked arrival and departure times, bought tickets, or confirmed reservations. Others sought the vending machines dispensing coffee or cold drinks. Some aimlessly examined papers and magazines, used the public telephones, hunted for taxis or rental cars, or simply stood in front of the huge windows to watch the runways.

Hallie wasn't interested in people-watching. She stopped at the first information booth she saw and asked, "Where do I pick up freight from Idaho?"

A perfectly groomed clerk told her, "Ramp four."

Trixie lagged behind Jim and Hallie. A family

moved ahead of her. At that moment, she faced the traveler at the nearest ticket window. She stopped in her tracks, letting Jim and Hallie go on without her. There was something so intriguingly familiar about the man that she crowded closer till she almost jostled his elbow. He was asking about an upstate flight schedule of the locally owned airline, known as the milk run because it hopped from one small airport to another. The clerk reached for a ticket and prepared to fill in the blanks where information was needed. Just then, the man looked back into Trixie's face. It was Miss Ryks's nephew.

"I've changed my mind," he told the clerk abruptly and quickly moved away, disappearing into a stream of people arriving from a north-south flight.

Taking care not to call attention to herself, Trixie moved away from the ticket window. She stationed herself on the far side of the flow of travelers to watch for Jim and Hallie. Even so, they startled her by returning from an unexpected direction. Jim carried a large brown cowhide suitcase exactly like the one Bobby had opened. Hallie was birthday-morning excited. "Clothes!" she cried. "Clothes that fit me!"

Jim grinned at this tall girl who could look him nearly straight in the eye.

"Good," said Trixie absentmindedly, still thinking about the man she'd just seen. All the way to the car, she kept a sharp lookout for Miss Ryks's nephew. Why had he changed his plans when he saw her? He'd never seen her before—she'd seen him.

Without being reminded, Jim turned at the Crab-apple Farm mailbox. He stopped the station wagon about halfway up the lane. "Is this spot okay?"

"I think," Trixie told him, "that this is just about the place where Reddy left the lane and dashed into the bushes. We're looking for any sign that something as heavy as a human being ran through here."

For some time, Jim, Hallie, and Trixie moved in and out of little cleared areas in the "wild garden" that hid the Belden lawn and flower gardens from Glen Road. At last, Trixie found a few wilted leaves on some twigs.

The three followed a trail of wilted and broken vegetation. Because of the time that had passed, some of the bushes had begun to revive, and the clues were hard to follow. Trixie's stubborn determination drove them on. It was Hallie who found a clear footprint on the soft shoulder of the road.

"Well," Trixie said, "now we know that Reddy chased a person, and it wasn't a girl."

"Unless she had very big feet," Jim said. "See? The shoe size is bigger than mine, so the man's probably taller than I am."

"Heavier, too," Trixie said.

"Let's check," Jim said. He walked several yards away from the road, then made a headlong dash across the shoulder. He left a print near the one that Hallie had found. Trixie sat on her heels to measure the depths of the two prints with a weed stem. The stem bent, but her eyes told her that the first print was deeper than the one Jim had made.

Several yards up the road, they found a place where the man might have stepped out of the lane of traffic to let a car pass. He had walked toward the Wheeler mailbox while Jim had driven in the opposite direction. Hallie decided he must have known the area.

"Not necessarily," Jim returned. "He could have hidden after Reddy quit barking. That would have given him a chance to see which way we were going."

As they walked back to the house to drop off the suitcase, Hallie reminded Trixie and Jim that Dan had been in the wagon and not in the bushes. "Thank goodness," Trixie answered, sounding prayerful.

On the way back to Manor House, Trixie fretted, "I wish we knew why Dan ran away and where he is."

Jim was sensible. "Whatever his reason, he's one worried young man. He knows that somebody took that ring from the desk and that he's under suspicion. It looks like the Belden-Wheeler partnership and the Bob-Whites have a job to do."

"I suppose that lets me out," Hallie sighed.

Trixie knew that Hallie liked Dan and wanted to help. "Of course it doesn't let you out," she declared. "The Bob-Whites will issue you a guest card the way they do at the country club." Jim, the Bob-White co-president, agreed.

"Well, then, when do we start?" Hallie asked.

"We've already started," Trixie answered. "We've proved that someone else could have taken Juliana's ring. Now, we have to find out how Dan got hold of it."

"I'll call Mart and Brian when we get home," Jim decided. "We'd better start a search for Dan."

When Jim drove into the porte cochere, Di and Honey whizzed alongside on bicycles. Honey shouted, "Miss Trask says all work and no play does you-know-what! Grab a bike and follow the leader!"

The bicycle rack stood near the servants' entrance. Trixie and Hallie scrambled out of the car and raced around the house. Hallie's legs were longer, and she was the first to reach the rack.

The only bicycle left for Trixie was Jim's ten-speed. She mounted it and caught up easily with the rest of the girls. Di was "it" and led the romp that ended at the clubhouse. As she dropped the kickstand of Jim's bicycle, Trixie was reminded of the similar blue bike at the inn.

Uh-oh. Had Jim gone to the inn that night, too? No. He'd been waiting at the lake. Di hadn't shared the evening swim, and neither had Dan. With a curl-bouncing shake of her blond head to clear her brain, Trixie hurried inside to join the fun of planning a shower for Juliana. With the mishmash of the Lynch robbery, Di's missing invitation, that aggravating wheelchair, Juliana's ring, and now Dan's disappearance, Trixie felt that she needed something calm and orderly to think about.

It had been Di's idea to give the party, so Trixie made her head of the planning committee, handing her the gavel. Honey began writing down names on an invitation list. Hallie didn't know anybody, so she just listened. Trixie found that she couldn't concentrate on the party plans after all. She turned to Honey and asked softly, "Who uses the bikes in the rack?"

Honey looked blank for an instant. "Lots of people —Jim, I, the maids, Regan—even Dad, if he wants to get somewhere in a hurry. There's lots of ground to cover when you run errands around here."

"Thanks. May I be excused for a few minutes?" Di looked startled but gave permission.

Trixie lost no time returning to the house. In the kitchen, she helped herself to a glass of milk as an excuse for being there. Trying to make her conversation about the bicycles sound casual was hopeless. The staff was familiar with the detective work by Honey and Trixie. Celia told her, "Maybe you'd best save your questions for Miss Trask." Trixie decided that she was right and returned to the clubhouse.

"Remember, not a word to Juliana!" Di warned when they had finished their plans. They rode back to the house. As Honey put her own bicycle in the rack, she said, "That's funny. The bicycle Dad usually rides is still missing."

"Still?" Trixie repeated alertly.

"Dad was going to use it Thursday morning, but it was gone, and he used Jim's instead. I remember because Jim wondered how he had put the first scratch on the blue paint."

"Did you mention that similar bike at the inn?" Trixie asked.

136

Honey said, "No. Should I have?"

"Search me," Trixie said, falling into step with Honey to follow Hallie and Di to the sewing room.

There Miss Trask was in command. A blond girl sat at the sewing machine. Heavy braids were wrapped around her head, like a crown, above a thin, pretty face. Warm brown eyes sparkled behind thick glasses. She flashed a bright smile, pausing in her work only long enough to repeat names when Miss Trask made introductions.

Her name was Ella Kline, and she did alterations for the Bride's Shop, as well as mending for Glen Road Inn, where she had a room. "Ella will live in while our project is in progress," Miss Trask said.

Just then, Ella needed something from the cutting table. She swung up painfully from her chair on crutches. At once, Trixie's mental computer did some calculating: Glen Road Inn plus Ella Kline—did that equal the elusive wheelchair?

Usually Trixie paid little attention to clothes and fidgeted over dressmaking demands on her time. Today she stood quietly on a platform during the careful fitting of a tissue pattern. Miss Trask noticed and congratulated her. For an instant, Trixie stared blankly, then told Miss Trask, "I'm thinking." After a few seconds, she looked down into Miss Trask's eyes and saw the curiosity there. With Ella within earshot, Trixie couldn't say, "Ella Kline needs a wheelchair, and I wonder if she ordered that one that was stolen."

Instead, Trixie gulped and asked, "Miss Trask, did

you manage to get in touch with Miss Ryks?"

"I still haven't been able to find her in," Miss Trask answered, then went back to her fitting.

"If you think Juliana would approve, we—"

"What am I to approve?" Juliana sang out, entering the room with a waltzing step. Her hands were full of envelopes, which she held up and let fall in a white flutter. "Everybody's coming! Isn't it wonderful?" Her golden tulip ring flashed its throatful of diamonds. Trixie knew that the day before she would have felt like dancing with Juliana. But now that ring reminded her of Dan. Where was he? Why had he run?

Juliana spun around to face Trixie. "What am I to okay?"

"Oh!" Trixie pushed the thought of Dan aside. She said hurriedly, "We wonder if you approve of our inviting Miss Ryks to your—"

Hallie loudly cleared her throat. To cover the slip Trixie had almost made, Honey interrupted, "—to tea to get acquainted before the wedding."

"So she won't feel strange and out of place," Di finished.

"That's a very kind suggestion," Juliana said.

Every girl in the room heaved a sigh of relief.

"Okay, then, how about Tuesday afternoon at our house?" Trixie said quickly.

"At two o'clock," Di put in. She added lamely, "I mean, that sounds like a very good time to meet a stranger. At two o'clock, I mean. On Tuesday."

"Yes," Juliana said, looking slightly dazed. "A very

good time. I'll be there, Trixie." As she left the room, she looked at Di and shook her head in bewilderment.

Trixie giggled. "Di, if Juliana asks why you're setting the time for my guests to call, just say that you're my new social secretary."

"Now, Trixie, what did you really mean to ask?" inquired Miss Trask.

"I only thought it might be a good idea to ask Miss Ryks to Juliana's shower. I'd be happy to deliver the invitation personally."

Trixie saw the disappointment in Hallie's black eyes before they were hidden by dark lashes. Quickly Trixie added, "Hallie and I could bike down to the inn after dinner. Okay, Hallie?"

Hallie's smile was the answer.

"That's an excellent idea," Miss Trask said. "Now, stand still, Trixie. I'm almost finished fitting this pattern."

When Hallie and Trixie reached home, Mrs. Belden was frying chicken for an early dinner. Peering into the skillet, Trixie asked, "One chicken for our mob, Moms? I thought you were baking a ham today."

"One chicken will serve five of us. The boys called. They're with Jim and are having supper with Mr. Maypenny," Mrs. Belden answered somewhat abstractedly. "I do wish I knew what's going on. I've lost a whole baked ham! I can't keep track of my own kitchen."

"Is there something I can do?" Trixie asked worriedly. It wasn't like her mother to get so upset.

"Hallie and I are supposed to take a shower invitation to Miss Ryks at the inn after dinner. Okay?"

"Fine!" Mrs. Belden exclaimed. "Just don't touch my cupboards!"

Bobby was sitting alone on the steps when the girls whizzed down the lane on bicycles. He waved. Trixie said, "Bobby's in some new phase. He hasn't been tagging after us lately."

"I kind of like it when he tags along," Hallie retorted. When they reached the inn, she headed for the back door. "Have to see my friend, the cook."

Trixie went in the front door, and to her surprise, the desk clerk recognized her. "Are you here to see Miss Ryks?"

"Yes, please, if she's in."

"I'm sure of it. Her nephew, Dick Ryks, passed by here a few minutes ago. He visited somebody up on the third floor before calling on his aunt."

The moustached nephew answered Trixie's tap on the door of room 214. Trixie introduced herself and explained about the shower. The man said he was Dick Ryks and took the invitation. "When is this shindig?" he asked.

"Tuesday," Trixie told him.

He shrugged. "I'll put Aunt Kate in a taxi. But you'll have to bring her back. I've got plans for that day."

Trixie promised Brian's jalopy for a taxi, then asked, "May I speak to her now?"

Dick shrugged again and chewed his ragged mous-

140

tache. "No can do. The old gal's asleep."

Neither Trixie nor the nephew mentioned their encounter at the airport. Trixie left by way of the service entrance and walked around the building to the kitchen door. There she found Hallie with a tall glass of lemonade in her hand. The cook was preparing an order that had just come in from room 214, while a maid waited at the table with Hallie.

As the cook handed the tray to the maid, Hallie bounced up. To Trixie's amazement, Hallie seemed to deliberately dump her lemonade all over the maid.

"I'm sorry," Hallie said. "Here. Give me your cap. I'll carry the tray while you change your uniform. Room two-fourteen, you said?" And she was on her way before the cook could voice any objection.

Hallie returned almost at once. She took off the cap, thanked the cook for the lemonade, and pulled Trixie out of the kitchen.

"Why'd you do such a rude thing?" Trixie demanded sternly.

Hallie's eyes widened enormously while she whispered, "Trixie, guess what! That tray was ordered for Miss Ryks, but she wasn't in the room! The bathroom door was open. There was no place to hide!"

"Gleeps!" Trixie gulped. "I just talked to that Dick Ryks and gave him the invitation. Wasn't he there either?"

"Oh, sure. He was sitting by the window in her wheelchair, with his feet on a table and a pile of magazines on the floor."

"I don't get it," Trixie admitted. "I want to stop at the desk for a minute. I have a question to ask that clerk."

The gossipy clerk looked surprised, and so did Hallie, when Trixie didn't mention Miss Ryks. Instead, she asked about Ella Kline.

"Yes," the clerk answered. "She has a room up on the third floor, but she isn't in right now. In fact, I believe she can't be reached for a week."

"I know," Trixie told him. "She's working for my friends the Wheelers. Sewing."

"That's what she does here," the clerk said.

"She must find it hard," Trixie said speculatively, "to manage her crutches on these slick stairs and halls. I would think she could get along better with a wheelchair like Miss Ryks has."

"Funny you should mention that," said the desk clerk. "Miss Ryks's chair is rented from Miss Kline. Since Miss Ryks will be with us such a short time, she didn't find it convenient to bring her own chair."

"A short time?" Trixie repeated.

The clerk laced his fingers and leaned over his high desk, all set to gossip. "I thought she might have told you that she's only with us through the first week in August."

"She'll be here for the wedding at the Wheelers?"

"I'm sure of it. She made quite a point of letting all of us know that she's well connected socially."

Trixie caught her breath. "Thank you," she said.

The clerk didn't seem to know what he was being

thanked for, but he said, "I'm sure you're welcome."

Trixie and Hallie left the desk hurriedly.

On their way out, they passed a pigeon-shaped, overdressed short woman, who was busily stripping bracelets and rings from her arms and hands. As she advanced on the reception desk, she gave orders to the clerk in a foghorn voice. "Take these up to the manager's safe, and tell him I won't be needing them for a few days!"

"Yes, Mrs. Boyer," the clerk said, holding out a plump hand. While the girls watched, Mrs. Boyer added a necklace and earrings to the glittering pile. When she went to the elevator, she looked like any middle-class housewife who had played bridge all afternoon.

Hallie gave a long whistle. "Do you suppose those diamonds are real?"

"You'd better believe it," Trixie said. "That's Mrs. Boyer. I've never met her face-to-face. She's got more money than the Wheelers and Lynches have put together!"

"And she lives *here?*" Hallie asked in amazement.

"She's eccentric," Trixie said.

As they pedaled up Glen Road, Trixie said, "I'm not sure exactly what information that clerk gave us."

"That Ella Kline was the one who ordered the chair in the first place," Hallie said.

"Yes. But how could Miss Ryks know that?"

"Maybe she already knew Ella Kline."

"We can check that with Ella. We don't know how

long Miss Ryks has been at the inn, but we know she'll be here for two more weeks—till the wedding."

"She's been here at least three days," Hallie mused. "She called Hans on Tuesday and gave her address as the inn."

"A fat lot of good that address does anyone. She's never *in*—or she's *in*disposed," Trixie grumbled.

"In the inn!" Hallie chanted. "I'd feel sick, too, if I had to look at that Dick Ryks all the time."

A Frog Hunter · 11

THE THREE BELDEN BOYS were sitting on the porch, saying nothing, doing nothing, when Trixie and Hallie arrived home. "We're waiting for Jim," Brian explained.

"But I thought you were with him," said Trixie. "Didn't you have supper with Mr. Maypenny?" She chose her words carefully because Mart was sending messages behind Bobby's back. Evidently Bobby didn't know that they'd been hunting for Dan.

Brian nodded and said, "I called Honey. She says that her parents haven't come home."

"And Sergeant Molinson didn't show up?" Hallie asked casually.

"She didn't mention him."

"Mrs. Wheeler must not have called him." Hallie turned to Trixie. "Is that good or bad?"

"Who knows? Who knows anything till we talk to Dan?" Trixie asked, ignoring Mart's signals.

"I talked to a man in the woods," Bobby said unexpectedly.

"Today?" Trixie demanded.

Bobby's sense of timing was not good. For him days came and days passed. "He was riding Jim's bike in the woods, and he had to stop quick or he'd have hit me. He said he was sorry he scared me."

"That's all he said?" Mart asked.

"That's talking," Bobby said with great dignity.

At that moment, Jim drove up the lane. Carrying a heavy flashlight, he walked to the porch. "You fellows feel like a hike?"

Bobby looked at the boots on Jim's feet and the jacket slung over a shoulder. "Are you going for a frog hunt?"

"Not exactly," Jim said cautiously. All eyes turned toward Bobby. One never knew what he had in mind.

"Well, neither was the man I saw. He said he was, but he didn't even know the way to the lake." Lately Bobby had learned to weigh his words. He explained carefully, "He did have a bag. No net, just a bag."

"When?"

"Where?"

"Who?"

Hallie's drawl climaxed the chorus. "Reckon there's

no sense in asking why. I know the answer. He wasn't hunting frogs." Her words and tone were kept light, but there was an undercurrent of tension in her voice.

Trixie and Hallie sat on the steps and watched the boys' flashlights bob through the dark woods like giant fireflies. "I wish . . ." Trixie sighed.

"You know we can't go," Hallie reminded her.

"Well, I certainly can't sleep till I know what's happened," Trixie retorted.

After giving permission for Trixie and Hallie to wait up for the boys, Mr. and Mrs. Belden went upstairs with Bobby. After a while, they turned off the lights that had made a big checkerboard design on the grass, and the lawn was dark. Reddy left his favorite grass nest and stretched his silky chin across Trixie's bare knees. She scratched his ears.

"I've been thinking," Trixie said soberly, "of all the things that Dan's been saying, like warning Juliana to take care of her ring, and wishing he could have prevented the Lynch robbery, and saying the ring hadn't been returned yet. It sounds like he did take that ring. If Mart, or Brian, or Jim took a valuable ring, they wouldn't know what to do with it, but Dan would. He lived by his wits on the streets of New York City."

"He has a good job and friends," Hallie pleaded. "What would cause him to slide backward?"

"I hope he didn't," Trixie said. "Trouble is, I can't tell my brain to shut up, and it keeps running facts through my computer. It says he could have taken the ring, but it doesn't tell me why."

"The footprint we found says that somebody else could have," Hallie reminded her cousin.

Trixie twisted her fingers together in a nervous tangle. "About Dan—sometimes we think we have a good reason for doing a wrong thing. Dan's as stubbornly loyal as Regan. It runs in their family." Trixie threw up her hands in helpless confusion. "When I think I'm on the right track, Bobby's frog hunter gets in the way. Dan may be out there in the woods with him."

"But he isn't a frog hunter," Hallie said soberly. Both girls stared at the night shadows.

To pass time, Trixie and Hallie went to the kitchen and baked oatmeal cookies. The last pan was hot from the oven when the three boys returned—tired, sleepy, and hungry. They hadn't found Dan, and Mr. Maypenny hadn't heard from him.

Trixie poured milk and passed around the cookies. Brian took one but hesitated before biting into it. "As far as Mr. Maypenny knows, Dan hasn't eaten all day."

"Did you see Bobby's frog hunter?" Trixie asked.

"No, but we did find some other trespassers. Remember Dan's old gang?" Brian asked. "Five of them were sacked out around the remains of a campfire where they'd cooked their supper."

Deeply troubled, Trixie said, "Did you wake them? You didn't, did you? That would have been a dangerous thing to do!"

"No," Jim assured her. "Afterward, we thought

maybe we should have, but there were five of them to our three. They could have come out of their sleeping bags with knives in their fists. They carry them."

"I know," Trixie whispered. "Do you suppose—" She broke off to listen to a sound that seemed to come from the backyard. She decided it had to be Reddy.

Jim finished Trixie's question: "—that Dan's gone back to the gang? We hope not, but it is possible."

Trixie could tell from her brothers' faces that the question had been discussed.

"We've decided to call the police," Brian said.

"No, Brian!" Trixie begged. "You'll just get Dan deeper in trouble if Mrs. Wheeler reported the recovery of the missing ring."

Gently Jim said, "Trix, how can he be in worse trouble? He's missing. He doesn't have his wallet, so he has no money. That means he's without food and shelter. As for that gang out there—whether Dan's with them or not, they spell danger. We have to call the police."

Tearfully, Trixie finally agreed. She listened while Brian talked to Sergeant Molinson. The last time Dan's gang had been in the area, Mr. Maypenny had been injured. Those teen-agers from the city played rough. When Brian hung up the phone, she asked, "Well, what did he say?"

"He says it's too soon to act, but he'll remain on the alert. No one's filed charges against the gang for trespassing, and there's no law against sleeping."

"Agreed!" Mart said wearily, and he stretched and

yawned widely. "We all need a good night's rest."

"Also, Dan hasn't been gone long enough to be considered a missing person. The sergeant's sorry that we're worried, and we're to keep him informed." Brian tousled Trixie's sandy curls. "He also asked about you, Trixie. He said, 'If Detective Belden's on the job, she'll know when she needs help.'"

Trixie was much too worried about Dan Mangan to take bows for either past or future performances. "What are we going to do about Dan?" she asked.

"Keep on looking for him till we find him," Brian answered. "What else?"

"We're getting up early," Mart said. "I'll set my alarm."

"Can we join you?" asked Hallie.

"No," said Brian. "We think it's far safer if you two keep a lookout for Dan around here till we see what that gang is up to."

After agreeing on a time to meet the Beldens the next day, Jim left for home.

Mart and Brian were preparing to resume their search for Dan when the rest of the Beldens got up Saturday morning. The radio was on, and suddenly a news item set nerves to tingling: "Police report an attempted break-in at Glen Road Inn. It would seem that the intended robbery victim was an elderly invalid. Because she was in a wheelchair, the guest couldn't reach her telephone before the burglar made his escape through a window. Authorities state that a local youth with a past record of juvenile offenses is reported missing and may possibly be involved. Now for the weather. . . ."

Trixie yelled, "I *told* you we shouldn't report Dan missing! Now see the trouble he's in!"

Brian turned off the radio with a forceful click. "We're doing what we can, in any way we can, to find Dan."

Hallie almost whispered, "Did anybody see and recognize Dan? Maybe he isn't in the woods. Maybe you're looking in the wrong place."

"That's possible," Mart agreed.

Mrs. Belden spoke with deep pity. "Dan could be in Timbuktu, and people would still suspect him after that report. They won't remember that he was a victim when he was in trouble before. First impressions aren't easily forgotten."

"My first impression was that I liked Dan," Hallie said loyally.

"Me, too," Bobby said, "but I don't like frog hunters. Frogs catch mosquitoes, and mosquitoes bite. So I think frogs belong where the mosquitoes are and not in moneybags."

Mr. Belden was a banker, and his children recognized the equipment used in a bank. He lowered his paper and asked, "What's that about a moneybag?"

Bobby mumbled through toast crumbs. "You can't put frogs in a moneybag. They can't breathe, and they dry out. But there was something in that bag."

Bobby suddenly became deaf when his father tried

to pursue the subject, so Trixie asked, "What does your frog hunter look like?"

"He has dirty feet," Bobby said. "Big ones. I couldn't see his eyes. He had black glasses on."

"Oh!" Trixie gasped. "I may know him. His aunt lives at Glen Road Inn. He probably got bored and left the inn for a while."

Bobby needed to think about that. When his tall brothers left the room, he said wistfully, "Nobody plays with me, or talks to me. Not even—"

"Not even who, Bobby?" Mrs. Belden asked.

"Not even Trixie," he finished mournfully. "I thought I was in a club, but I'm not. Nobody talks to me. Sometimes I need to talk." He turned to Hallie. "Okay if I borry Cap's nocklers? I'm going to climb a tree and see what that frog hunter is doing today."

"Help yourself, Bobby," Hallie answered.

When they were told about the news release, Regan, Tom, and Mr. Maypenny left their regular work and joined the search for Dan. Using horses, bicycles, the station wagon, and Brian's jalopy, they combed the district. No one had seen Dan, but many had heard the news report. Regan revealed to the Bob-Whites that he hadn't had time to mention the ring before Dan ran.

Trixie fretted over that information. "It may mean that Dan ran *to* somebody else instead of *away from* Regan."

"Yes," Honey agreed, "but that scares me."

During the search, the girls found scraps of time to

work with Mrs. Belden and Mrs. Lynch on preparations for Juliana's shower. Invitation acceptances were arriving in the mail. Mrs. Belden didn't think it wise to cancel the party because Dan was missing. She pointed out that the police were now on the job.

Hallie wondered if they should invite Mrs. Boyer to the party, but Mrs. Belden was all aflutter at the very idea of having her in the house. "Mrs. Boyer? Oh, my, no! I'd be afraid to have all those diamonds here with that gang loose in the game preserve."

Each day brought wedding gifts to Manor House, where Ella and Miss Trask were able to carry on the sewing project without much help from the girls. Regan and Tom built a bower that they would carry to the garden to be covered with flowers and greenery. Individually and as a group, the Bob-Whites made frequent trips to see Mr. Maypenny. The old gamekeeper was worried and lonely.

In this already overcrowded time, Bobby needed attention. His scooter disappeared, and so did Cap's "nocklers." "I know where I left 'em by the tree, an' they're not there," he mourned.

But neither were some other things "there." The bicycle Matthew Wheeler liked to use hadn't been found, and on the night before the shower, the rest of the Manor House bicycles disappeared. Only Jim's ten-speed remained. Up at the stone house, the Lynches lost bicycles, tricycles, scooters, and wagons. Other Glen Road children lost their "wheels," too. These disappearances added to Honey and Trixie's list of mysteries to be investigated.

Tuesday was a bright, cloudless day. Juliana's shower was held in the backyard. Mart and Brian had set up picnic tables and benches. All the neighbors shared their garden flowers, and solid masses of golden-hearted white daisies covered the worn spots in the grass where Bobby had played his games and Reddy had dug to find a cool bed.

Exactly at two o'clock, Juliana arrived at the front door, unaware that the backyard was already filled with friends. She told Trixie, "I do hope Miss Ryks knew my parents. Ever since she called Hans, I've been anxious to meet her."

"So have I," Trixie confessed. "I've tried twice to see her. Sometimes I wonder if there is such a person!" Trixie looked down the lane. "But there must be. Here comes a taxi."

Trixie tried not to stare at the very old, stately woman, who waited in the front seat until the driver removed her collapsible wheelchair from the back-seat. Although the day was hot, Miss Ryks's outfit had long sleeves, a high tight collar with a fluff of lace, and a full skirt that covered her feet. Blue white hair was piled high on her head in an elaborate arrangement. Her eyes were concealed by large sunglasses sitting firmly on a rather large nose.

Miss Ryks leaned heavily on the driver's arm while stepping from the taxi to the wheelchair. In that brief glimpse of the woman's upright figure, Trixie received the impression of a body with shoulders wider than hips. Yet when Miss Ryks settled into her chair, her shoulders hunched, and she no longer seemed either tall or strong. It was all very confusing.

Her voice was deep and breathy, but thin, as if something crowded her windpipe. It seemed that every word she spoke took great effort. A large, bony hand, covered with rings, patted Trixie's bare arm. Wheezily she said, "You can't be little Juliana. You're too—"

"Too big?" Trixie finished with a rueful smile. "You're right. I'm your hostess, Trixie Belden." Juliana ran lightly down the steps and across the grass. "And this is Juliana."

"My dear" was all Miss Ryks had to say. And she didn't utter another word during all the flurry of meeting Mrs. Belden, Hallie, Di, and Mrs. Lynch. She simply nodded in a regal manner that required no speech.

Juliana allowed herself to be led to the backyard by Mrs. Belden, while Trixie pushed the wheelchair. Miss Ryks might be frail, but she wasn't exactly lightweight.

"Surprise, surprise!" cried smiling guests, crowding around Juliana.

Juliana sparkled. She danced from person to person, chanting, "I'm so glad you're here. How delightful!" She stopped in front of Miss Trask and Honey to tease, "I thought you two had errands to run!"

Everybody was there, from Mrs. Vanderpoel to Di's small twin sisters. Di's careful plans became happy

155

reality filled with good humor, warm conversation, delicious food, and beautiful gifts for the bride-to-be. As Trixie moved among the guests, she noticed that Mrs. Vanderpoel had made herself Miss Ryks's champion, even to the point of volunteering to pick her up for the wedding. "Mr. Lytell is taking me, and I'm sure he'll be happy to include you."

Trixie received the decided impression that Miss Ryks didn't wish to be included, but Mrs. Vanderpoel insisted. "And you must have tea with me. I'll invite Juliana and Mrs. Wheeler, too."

This time Miss Ryks flatly refused. "I can't always be sure of the condition of my health," she wheezed.

Trixie was more concerned about the state of the woman's manners. After having made such a point of being asked to the wedding, Miss Ryks was making no effort to get acquainted with Juliana.

The tiny Dutch girl sat beside Miss Ryks and asked questions that might uncover the relationship between them. She got nowhere with Miss Ryks. The ancient dowager crouched in her chair and played with the many rings on her fingers. She wore several long strands of pearls and repeatedly tied them in knots, then untied them. Her hands were never still.

Trixie wished she could see the eyes above that big nose. "I'll bet she doesn't miss a thing," she whispered to Di while they served the cake.

"I'll call on you," Mrs. Vanderpoel promised Miss Ryks as she left.

"To be sure," Miss Ryks agreed without enthusiasm.

Brian was pressed into service to return Miss Ryks to the inn, and Jim had the happy chore of taking home Juliana and all her gifts, tissue paper, and ribbons. Trixie was torn between going with Brian and staying for one last look at the presents. Brian made the choice for her. "I'll need help with the wheelchair," he said.

At the inn, Miss Ryks wheezed, "I'm tired. I must get to my room."

Trixie expected Dick Ryks to appear at the door of room 214, but he didn't. Still, as Trixie turned away from the room and followed Brian down the hall, she heard the nephew's nasal voice. "How was the shindig, Aunt Kate?" Miss Ryks's answer was muffled.

"That's funny," Trixie said. "Where did he come from?"

Brian shrugged. He thought Dick might have been in the bathroom when they got there.

"Yes," Trixie agreed. "That was the only place he could have been."

When Trixie and Brian reached the Crabapple Farm lane, Bobby was sitting near the mailbox, and Brian stopped to give him a ride to the house. In the car, Bobby slumped in the backseat, totally woebegone.

"Got problems?" Brian inquired seriously.

Bobby sighed loudly. "It's my scooter. You know, Brian, a guy just can't live without his wheels."

Brian knew. Nothing had seemed as important to him as the purchase of his jalopy. "I'll help you hunt for it as soon as we put away the tables and chairs. Okay?" Bobby sniffed loudly.

Trixie hugged him. "I'll help, too."

Even Mr. and Mrs. Belden joined in the search. Beldens moved out over the whole farm till they had covered all the places Bobby ever played. But—no scooter.

Trixie called the Lynches. Di reported that servants, and family, too, had been unable to find a trace of all the missing "wheels" at their house. The same report came from Honey.

"Have you called the police?" Trixie asked Honey. "We didn't because one beat-up scooter wasn't valuable enough to bother the sergeant about—"

Trixie was interrupted by a howl from Bobby. "*Bother!*" He ran from the room, sobbing, "Moms, Trixie says I'm a bother!"

"I'll call you back, Honey," Trixie said hastily. "But —did you call the police?" The answer was yes.

Teed's and Wheels · 12

CRABAPPLE FARM couldn't be neglected, and neither could the preparations for Juliana's wedding and the search for Dan. Trixie had never felt more frustrated —there just weren't enough days in the week or hours in each day. Bobby's gloom settled over the Belden homelife like smog in a valley.

In the Wheeler stable, Regan was silent and withdrawn. Mr. Maypenny quit cooking for himself and spent all his time riding old Spartan on the crisscross of trails in the game preserve. Miss Trask had his food delivered from Manor House, and both Trixie and Di brought him snacks from their homes when they visited his cottage daily.

With loving concern, the Bob-Whites tried to keep problems from dampening Juliana's joy. The bower was set in the garden, between the birdbath and the summerhouse. Gifts were received and entered in the bride's record book. Juliana was already writing her thank-you notes and packing trunks. The cook was making festive foods and storing them in the freezers.

Ella Kline worked alone in the sewing room most of the time. She was looking forward to returning to her room at the inn.

"Will you get your wheelchair back?" Trixie asked.

Ella smiled. "Yes. And the money from Miss Ryks will take care of my first payment."

"Did you know Miss Ryks before she came to the inn?" Trixie asked.

"No," Ella answered. "I talked to her nephew about the wheelchair. As a matter of fact, I've never seen her, but I did see her stretcher carried to room two-fourteen. It's unusual to have an ambulance arrive at the inn, and everybody watched. I got the impression of a scrawny little person."

"Scrawny? Little?" Trixie was amazed. Watching Miss Ryks get out of the taxi, Trixie had thought that she had broader shoulders and was taller than most women. Her hands were large, and so was her nose. Trixie couldn't wait to discuss this with Honey and Hallie.

Yet when Trixie did see Honey, neither of them mentioned Miss Ryks. They could only worry about Dan. Had he gone back to the streets of the city?

Had he been kidnapped? Was he lying hurt—or worse
—in the forest? Sergeant Molinson was checking on
all of those possibilities.

In their sleuthing, none of the boys had been able
to turn up a real clue, though they did report having
seen strange boys hanging around. The strangers wore
cowboy boots like those Dan had worn when he first
came to the area. One boy—the shortest, scrawniest
one of the group—wore a western-style hat shoved
back on his head. Jim said, "I suppose he thinks it
makes him look tougher."

Trixie almost tripped over that same young man's
boots one afternoon when she went into Wimpy's. He
was wearing the hat and staring through the window
at the alley beyond the parking lot.

Trixie stared in the same direction. There was the
usual clutter of jalopies and family vehicles in the
parking lot, but the boy wasn't looking at these. His
head was turned toward a Teed pickup truck pulling
out of the alley.

When the truck turned the corner, the boy made
an okay sign with his finger and thumb and clumped
out of the room. He was followed by four older boys,
all wearing the same kind of cowboy boots.

Trixie hurried to the booth where the Bob-Whites
and Hallie sat. In a loud whisper, she said, "They were
here! Dan's gang!"

"We saw them." Jim spoke for Brian and Mart as
well as himself. The three looked tired. Trixie knew
that her brothers were steadily losing both sleep and

161

appetite, and she suspected the same was true of Jim.

"That truck . . ." Hallie said cautiously. After Trixie's outburst in the parking lot, Teed's had been a taboo subject. "Did you see what it was carrying?"

Nobody had noticed.

"Bicycles," Hallie said. "Lots of them, and they didn't look new."

"What!" Jim jumped up. "Let's go!"

The Bob-Whites made a pell-mell dash for the station wagon.

Two blocks from Wimpy's, the Teed truck had stopped at the bottom of a slope for a red light. When the light changed, Jim saw which direction the truck headed and followed it as fast as the speed limit allowed. His passengers kept track of the pickup as it moved through traffic.

When they found themselves on the White Plains highway, Trixie asked anxiously, "Do we have enough gas?"

"I just filled up," Jim said. "I can go as far as he can, and I can use a credit card to get home."

On the open road at last, Jim was able to pass enough cars to come within easy view of the Teed truck. It was a pickup with a boxlike frame added to carry bulky but lightweight freight. Bicycles standing in neat rows were clearly visible.

Unexpectedly, the truck turned off on a two-lane road. Now the group began to worry about the wild-goose chase they might be on. Within a mile or two, something new was added along the roadside. Hand-lettered signs appeared that read, YARD SALE! BIKES, TRIKES, SCOOTERS, WAGONS. STRAIGHT AHEAD!

The Teed truck stopped at an ordinary-looking country home. A banner stretched across the front porch proclaimed that yard to be the site of the sale. Several cars were parked in the driveway and along the edges of the road.

"Customers already!" Trixie gasped.

"There must have been an ad in the paper," Honey said, "or they wouldn't have known when and where to come."

Jim parked at an angle behind the pickup. When Di told him that the truck wouldn't be able to get out, Jim grinned. "That's the idea, Di. Come on. Let's mingle while they unload."

The driver was the same talkative man who had lost the wheelchair. A second man hopped from the truck and began to help unload the bicycles. Jim scowled. "There's Dad's bike."

"Mine, too!" Honey said.

"And there's Bobby's scooter!" Trixie exploded.

"The twins' wagons," Di added, then gasped, "and our furniture!" The bicycles had hidden the neatly packed furniture that was now being unloaded.

"Ssh!" Brian warned. "These people may be in cahoots with the thieves. We've got to get to a phone and call Sergeant Molinson."

"It's out of his district," Mart objected.

Trixie argued, "He'll tell us what to do!"

"I can't use the phone here," Jim said. "I'll have to

go back to that house we just passed. Cause any kind of commotion you have to, but don't let anyone buy anything!"

Jim walked down the road while the Bob-Whites moved among the stolen items. Each time a customer became interested in an article, a Bob-White crowded forward to examine it, too. It became impossible for the customers to concentrate on buying.

Under the banner on the porch, a teen-ager sat at a table with a cash till ready for use. He wore cowboy boots. Anxiously Trixie kept watch to see if anybody else wore the high-heeled boots, but she saw no one who did. She kept a firm grip on Bobby's scooter, even when a red-faced young mother tried to buy it for her whining five-year-old.

The crowd was getting cranky, and so was the pickup driver. "Oh, boy! Oh, boy!" Hallie gasped. "We're in everybody's hair. Cap and Knut will never believe this."

The Teed man, having unloaded his freight, tried to get out of the driveway. When he backed up his truck, the station wagon's nose was against the truck bed. When he tried to move forward to circle the house, other cars and Hallie on a bicycle blocked the way.

The driver pleaded. He argued, and he yelled. "Look, sis, I gotta get back on the job! I gotta punch a time clock, see? Say, don't I know you? I've seen you someplace!"

Brian managed to be here, there, and everywhere,

and so did Mart. They were so "helpful" that a fat woman in slacks complained loudly, "I never heard of such a mismanaged yard sale! Here come the police. It's about time!"

"Good!" Trixie shouted to Honey. "Jim's with them, so they're on our side."

"We hope!" Honey retorted.

Two policemen came up the drive with Jim. They blew their whistles and shouted, "Nobody's to leave the yard!"

Trixie saw the booted teen-ager try to slip inside the house, and she shrieked, "He's getting away!" A long-legged policeman managed to catch up with him.

The other officer was questioning the Teed driver closely. The driver raised his voice to plead, "Look! Somebody up there doesn't like me, see? A couple weeks ago, I got in the doghouse with my boss. One more run-in, and I'm gonna get fired, see? I ain't got nothin' to do with no robbery. I just took my slip from the desk. I loaded my truck, and I brung it out here, see? I've never been in police trouble, I swear."

Wearily the policeman told him, "I have orders to see that you pack up your load and deliver it to the police station in Sleepyside, and that's what we're going to do. Get a move on."

He turned. "Is one of you named Trixie Belden? Well, Sergeant Molinson wants to talk to you."

The Bob-Whites had done their job well. Not one penny lay in the cash till on the porch. Disappointed customers grumbled as they got into their cars and left the yard sale. The relieved Bob-Whites headed toward Sleepyside.

Honey sighed. "I hope that closes this case, so we can go on with the wedding preparations."

Trixie hoped so, too, but she was not convinced that they had done any more than scratch the surface of the mystery. True, one gang member had been caught. But where were the rest of them? Who was their leader? Was Dan back with the gang, and where was he?

In Sleepyside, Jim drove straight to the police station, where they found Sergeant Molinson waiting for a full report. The sullen teen-ager, sitting in the sergeant's office, muttered, "My boss'll fix you kids for this. He can, you know!"

"Boss!" Trixie cried. "I knew there had to be a leader. They're too young to organize a large-scale theft and an out-of-town sale."

Sergeant Molinson grinned. "I don't know about that. You Bob-Whites aren't in wheelchairs yet, and you do pretty well on your projects."

Wheelchairs, Trixie thought. *That word again.* She asked wistfully, "Have you found Dan?"

"Not a sign of him, but we'll keep in touch," the sergeant promised. "Have your folks come around to identify their property. Anybody care to identify and remove this scooter?" He raised an eyebrow at Trixie.

"I do!" Trixie exclaimed. "Bobby will think Santa

came in August instead of December this year."

On August fourth, just two days before the wedding, Miss Trask called all of the girls to the sewing room for a final fitting of their dresses. Even Mrs. Wheeler came to help Honey, Di, Hallie, and Trixie put on the lovely white dresses.

Tom had built a sturdy stand to make it easier for Ella to do fittings. When it was Trixie's turn to be checked, she stepped up onto the stand. Ella, her crutches beside her, sat comfortably on the floor, adjusting Trixie's hem. Mrs. Wheeler sat in a rocking chair, ready to give final approval.

Feeling like a fairy-tale princess, Trixie swirled the deep, lace-edged ruffle around her ankles. When she faced the triple mirrors, she could see that she looked as pretty as she felt. She smoothed the blue ribbon that fitted snugly around a waist that looked almost as tiny as Di's. There hadn't been time for many trips to Wimpy's lately, and the results showed on her figure.

Miss Trask said, "Turn. A little more. There. That's right. Now, stand still."

Trixie stood. From her perch on the little platform, she could look through the window and down on the bicycle rack, where all the Wheeler bicycles were now in place. The children were happy at the Lynch and Belden houses because they had their scooters, wagons, and bikes again, and the furniture was back in the Lynch family room. Here at Manor House, errands could be run as usual. In fact, someone was

167

taking a bike as Trixie watched.

She gasped and leaned forward, receiving a sharp "Stand still!" from Miss Trask.

The bike being taken was Jim's, and the thief was that scrawny little teen-ager who wore both a cowboy hat and boots! He was stealing the bike in broad daylight!

Trixie unzipped her white dress as fast as she could, while Miss Trask stood back, too startled to scold. Trying to keep her balance as she pulled on her shorts, Trixie saw the boy pedal toward the stable at a furious pace. Buttoning her blouse as she ran, Trixie pell-melled from the house. She had no idea what she was getting into as she swung astride Honey's unlocked bike and took off.

At the stable, a tread mark showed that the thief had gone straight through the alleyway. He knew where he was going. Behind the stable, the only possible route was the path to the woods, and Trixie took it. Once on that, the ride was all downhill. The path was well cleared, but it took all of Trixie's skill to negotiate the curves at the speed she was traveling. Several times, she almost fell. Once she was stabbed by conscience, remembering the promise she had made to her brothers not to go off alone. There was no time to worry about that now.

The path led across Crabapple Farm. Reddy barked when she passed behind the shed. Bobby's voice came out of a tree: "Everybody's in a hurry!" Well, that meant that he'd seen the scrawny kid. Trixie didn't slow down. She pedaled even more furiously.

The path paralleled Glen Road and led in a round-about curve to the inn. She knew she'd gain time by taking to the road, but the scrawny teen-ager might swerve onto a bypath at any point. As fast as she'd ridden, Trixie knew that he hadn't had time to stop and hide the bike. Still, she couldn't see him anywhere.

Feeling let down, Trixie circled the parking lot at the inn, then rode down the sidewalk near the kitchen. There! In the same lilac hedge where it had been hidden before was Jim's ten-speed. That meant the thief was around someplace.

Trixie had a sudden idea—Bobby's frog hunter had sounded like that messy-looking Dick Ryks! He, too, had been seen in the woods. Maybe, just maybe, that teen-ager was making contact with Dick. That meant Miss Ryks's room. And if not there, perhaps a room up on the third floor where Dick was said to visit.

Trixie left Honey's bicycle in the inn's rack. When she walked toward the building entrance, she saw Mr. Lytell's car pull into the parking lot, with Mrs. Vanderpoel waving from the front seat. Trixie grinned, remembering Miss Ryks's lack of enthusiasm about company calling. Well, that lady was about to have more company than she bargained for.

As usual, it was the nephew who answered Trixie's tap at room 214. Before she could say a word, he slammed the door in her face. Angrily Trixie raised her hand to pound on the door, then stopped. Miss Ryks's room was on the ground floor. It might be possible to look into that room from outside and see if the bicycle thief was in there.

Trixie hurried out the service entrance and passed the garbage cans. Two more of the Wheeler bicycles leaned against the brick wall. Honey and Hallie could be here! Now, where were they hiding?

Trixie found her cousin and her best friend behind the lilac hedge near Miss Ryks's windows. "Why did you come here?" she demanded.

"Haven't I always spied on you?" Hallie teased.

Honey said, "We knew that path led to the inn, so we came down the road. We could make better time."

Hallie crouched and spread the lilac branches apart for a peephole. "What's going on in there? First the room was empty. After a while, a man came in and flopped in a chair and put his feet up. Then he opened the door."

"Isn't Miss Ryks in there?"

"Not unless that Dick locked her in the bathroom. The wheelchair's empty, and so's the bed."

Through sheer curtains at the closed windows, Trixie could see the dim outlines of a chair and a bed. She could also make out Dick Ryks, but not the scrawny teen-ager.

"Look," Hallie said. "He's getting a phone call."

"Mrs. Vanderpoel must be calling from the desk!" Trixie said. "I saw her in the parking lot."

After a long silence, Hallie gasped, "Trixie! Dick

went into the bathroom, but Miss Ryks came out!"

"She couldn't have. You must have seen her come from the hall."

"No! The hall door didn't open. Look, there she is, and she's *walking!*"

Miss Ryks strode about the room with great vigor, followed by clouds of smoke. "She's smoking a cigar!" Honey said with distaste.

At that moment, Miss Ryks stooped slightly to look into a mirror, patted her blue white hair, and put a choker around her throat. "No wonder she can't talk," Hallie said. "She chokes herself."

Next, Miss Ryks put on her dark glasses, threw a big scarf over her shoulders, strode briskly to her wheelchair, and hunched herself into place. "That old fraud!" Trixie stormed. "She's no cripple, and Ella Kline needs that chair."

When the door opened, the visitor was indeed Mrs. Vanderpoel. After a little head-nodding conversation, Miss Ryks reached for the telephone. "She must be ordering tea," Trixie said. "Excuse me. I'll be right back."

Within minutes, Trixie was back to ask, "What now?"

Honey told her, "Miss Ryks pretended to be too weak to answer the door without help, so Mrs. Vanderpoel pushed her chair. The maid was at the door with a note. Miss Ryks reached for it, but she gave it to Mrs. Vanderpoel. Now Mrs. Vanderpoel keeps looking this way. What did you do, anyway?"

"I sent Mrs. Vanderpoel a message that we're out here," Trixie replied. "I asked her to feel faint so that Miss Ryks would have to call for Dick's help."

Miss Ryks's back was to the windows. Mrs. Vanderpoel fanned her face and changed chairs. "She must be telling Miss Ryks that she needs air," Hallie said.

Trixie agreed, then muttered, "I hope Miss Ryks can't see us in that mirror."

Mrs. Vanderpoel stared straight out the windows and swooned out of her chair. For a while, the figure in the wheelchair didn't move. Then, she stood up, strode to the bathroom, and came back with a glass of water. She didn't offer it to Mrs. Vanderpoel but instead sloshed the water in her face! Next, she slumped into the wheelchair as if she herself needed help.

Mrs. Vanderpoel slowly staggered to her feet. In a few minutes, the maid brought a tray and set it on the chest of drawers. However, Mrs. Vanderpoel didn't stay to tea.

The girls raced to the front door, where they found their plump friend sopping the front of her dress with a handkerchief. "My land, what was that all about?" she asked them.

"We'll tell you later," Trixie answered. "Quick, did she leave the bathroom door open?"

"Well, yes, she did."

"Was her nephew hiding in the bathroom?"

"No. There was only Miss Ryks, and, my dears, do you know that surprising woman can walk when she cares to make the attempt?" Tut-tutting, she headed for the parking lot and Mr. Lytell's car.

The girls returned to the rear of the building for the bicycles Hallie and Honey had left there. Suddenly Trixie warned, "Ssh! Get down! Look who's here now!"

It was the scrawny teen-ager! He was being pulled through the window of room 214 by Miss Ryks.

"I'll bet *that's* who came in on the stretcher," Trixie said shrewdly. "Ella said little and scrawny, and he sure is. Agreed?"

Two heads nodded. Hallie added, "And now we know who was seen sneaking out of Miss Ryks's window. I knew it wasn't Dan."

Trixie picked up on Hallie's thought and said, "Maybe Dan found out what they were up to, and they blamed it on him to get him in trouble with the police and keep him out of their hair."

"J-Just blamed him, that's all?" Honey quavered. "What do you suppose they're up to, anyway? I'm sure it has to be connected with the robberies, now that I see that gang member here."

"Will you look at that!" Hallie burst out. "Now Miss Ryks is walking around with her nephew's head on!"

"It's—it's a wig!" Trixie gasped. "That person in room two-fourteen is a man! He does it with wigs— a white one when he's Miss Ryks, and that moth-eaten thing when he's Dick."

As the girls watched through the window, the person in room 214 dropped Miss Ryks's dress to the floor

173

and strode about in hiphugger jeans. "I'll bet he's barefoot, too," Trixie said, shuddering. "Let's get out of here. I'm scared."

"Me, too," whispered both Honey and Hallie.

On their bikes again, they rode beyond the parking lot, then rested in the shade. For a long moment, not a word was said. Wide-eyed with excitement, Trixie said, "Dick is Bobby's frog hunter, I'm pretty sure. Nobody else we know goes around barefoot and wearing dark glasses. But Dick is also his own aunt and has contact with Dan's old gang. I saw that scrawny kid give the okay sign to the gang at Wimpy's, and we just saw him yanked through that window. You're right, Honey. They are a gang of thieves."

"All the robberies have to be tied together because the Lynch furniture was at the yard sale with the bikes," Hallie chimed in. "The 'Early Kids' note involved the country club where that comic was working the night the Lynch mansion was robbed."

"That clinches it!" Trixie exclaimed. "Oliver Tolliver, the comic, quit right after that news story. That same day, he showed up at the inn as Miss Ryks. When he, or she, moved in, the skinny kid was on the stretcher playing Miss Ryks, and Oliver was in that brassy wig playing the role of Dick Ryks till he could get to room two-fourteen and change his clothes. He's an actor, and he has costumes and makeup. He can be anybody he chooses to be."

"Pretty slick," Hallie said. "At the country club, he could decide who he wanted to rob—"

"—and send the gang out to do it," Trixie finished. "The club even provided the stationery for the notes he wrote! Do you realize what we're saying? Miss Ryks is the gang's boss! That kid that got arrested said the boss would get even with us, and Miss Ryks is coming to the wedding. Oh-h-h . . ." Trixie moaned. "What's she, I mean he, going to do?"

"We'll talk to Dad," Honey advised. "We'll ask him to have Sergeant Molinson's men there. It'll look like they're guarding the wedding gifts."

Soberly, the girls pedaled home, aware at last that the game Miss Ryks was playing was for keeps.

Within sight of the Belden mailbox, Trixie warned, "Until Dan's found, we have to walk on eggshells."

Hallie sighed heavily. "And I've got big feet."

The Truth Seeker · 13

SICK WITH WORRY, Trixie was afraid to speak and afraid not to speak. The rest of the day, she tried desperately to make plans but always faced a blank wall. How could she plan protection for her friends and family when she didn't know what that crook had in mind? It was just one more day till the wedding. In that time, anything might happen.

That night, Mrs. Belden stayed in the kitchen long after dinner to prepare dough for the next day's bread baking. "Sometimes I think I'm feeding two families," she scolded good-naturedly. "How do all of you eat so much and stay so thin?"

"Me? Thin?" Trixie asked hopefully.

Mart hooted. "Dream on, sweet princess!"

"That's just what I'm going to do," Trixie retorted.

Bobby followed Trixie to her room and stood in the doorway, waiting to be invited in to talk. Trixie coaxed, "Later, please, Bobby?" She felt guilty when he turned away, walking like a little old man. What was bothering him? She'd find out just as soon as the wedding was over and Dan was found.

The following afternoon, Miss Trask directed the wedding rehearsal in the garden. Not one detail had been overlooked. The ceremony would be perfect but for one thing—an usher was missing. Peter Belden substituted for Dan. The day Trixie had awaited with so much excitement was overcast with a gloom she couldn't shake. The Bob-Whites smiled, but their eyes were too bright, their voices too sharp, and their movements too nervous.

Trixie didn't have much appetite and left most of her dinner on her plate. Quite late, she awoke from a restless sleep. At first, she thought hunger had roused her. Then, she noticed that the light was on in the hall. Fully expecting to find Brian or Mart raiding the refrigerator, she tiptoed to the kitchen.

"Bobby!" she gasped. "What are you doing up in the middle of the night?"

Wide-eyed with fright, Bobby spun around. In one hand, he held a slice of bread, in the other, a knife globbed with peanut butter. On the counter stood a pitcher of milk and other sandwich-making materials.

Trixie thought she heard Reddy and moved toward

a window. Bobby tensed, then cried, "Don't go close to the window, please, Trixie!"

"Bobby," Trixie whispered, "what's wrong?"

"D-Don't even look at the window. Or the telephone," Bobby begged. "S-Smile at me? Pretend you're hungry, please, Trixie?" Bobby's mouth curved in a bright smile, but it didn't match his quavering voice.

"Okay." Trixie, too, made a sandwich. She whispered, "Who's out there, Bobby?"

"Those robber kids," Bobby said. "They sleep in our shed at night, and they wait for me to feed them."

"Bobby!" Trixie gasped.

"Ssh!" the small boy warned fiercely. "They'll hurt Reddy with their knives if I tell anybody about them or call the police. And they'll hurt Dan, too. They've got the nocklers, and they always watch me." He gulped and made another sandwich. "I was trying to tell you before, Trixie, but you didn't have time."

"Oh, I'm sorry, honey!" Trixie shivered with his fright added to her own. "Do they know we have three telephones?"

"I don't think so," Bobby muttered.

"I'll go upstairs and call the police. You go right on doing what they told you to do. Okay?"

"Okay," Bobby said.

Trixie made herself take time to pour milk and drink it, then she hugged Bobby and left the room. *Oh, please, hurry!* she prayed, waiting for her telephone call to go through.

She found the police station in an uproar. The police had been called to Glen Road Inn, and she finally contacted Sergeant Molinson there.

"We need you at Crabapple Farm, sir!" she begged. "Bobby's in danger! It's that gang!"

"Be right there," Sergeant Molinson promised.

Trixie went back downstairs and stood in the dark, watching Bobby without being seen. This whole nightmare had begun when Bobby used the "nocklers." Now Cap's "nocklers" watched Bobby. Suddenly, she realized that Bobby was being watched just as she had watched Miss Ryks. This invasion of privacy was a matter of viewpoint! She much preferred being the watcher instead of the one being watched.

During the heart-thumping wait for the police, Trixie forgave Bobby for every aggravating thing he'd ever done or said. She prayed for his safety as he went out the kitchen door with the food.

When she was sure she heard a motor, she ran through the dark house and out the front door. The sergeant had wisely approached without using headlights. She rushed to him, sobbing under her breath, and quickly told him what was happening.

"When Bobby comes back in the house, lock the door and turn off the lights," the sergeant instructed her. "My men will take care of rounding up this gang."

It was a good plan, but it didn't work. Trixie waited, but Bobby didn't come back in the house. When she could stand the waiting no longer, she went after him.

The instant Trixie opened the kitchen door, she was grabbed. She just had time to scream, as only she could scream, before a voice growled, "Shut up, or you've had it!" A hand was clamped over her mouth.

Mart's and Brian's rooms were above the kitchen area. Trixie's cry awakened them, and they pounded down the stairs. Lights flashed on in the guest room, then upstairs where Mr. and Mrs. Belden slept. Out of the dark came the police.

Pajamas, police badges, cowboy boots, flashlights, and Reddy jumbled together in a terrifying game of hide-and-seek in and out of the shadows, through the house, around the shed, and into the garden.

In the midst of the pandemonium, Trixie bit the hand on her mouth, butted hard with her head, and ran for the shed. "Bobby!" she screamed. "Where are you?"

"They're holdin' me!" Bobby wailed.

Just as Trixie reached Bobby, a pair of arms reached for her. She kicked, screamed, and fought them off until a stern voice boomed, "Trixie Belden! This is Sergeant Molinson!" Trixie calmed down, and the sergeant turned his flashlight on the interior of the shed.

"There's nobody else here. They got away!" she exclaimed.

"Did you expect them to hang around?" the sergeant grumbled. "Our birds have flown the coop."

"This time I don't care!" Trixie cried. "Bobby's safe!" Her arms went around his shoulders, and she gently led him back to the house.

Usually Bobby's tears were minimal, squeezed out for effect. This time the tears gushed down his cheeks.

Mr. and Mrs. Belden stared in amazement at their children and Sergeant Molinson, standing in an awkward row in the farmhouse kitchen.

"What in the world is happening here?" Mrs. Belden demanded.

Bobby told his story. He'd found the gang in the woods. They'd let him join their "secret club," and it was always his turn to bring refreshments. It was fun until he saw they had Di's doughnut-shaped radio. When they wouldn't let him take it back to her, he realized that they were the ones who had robbed the Lynch house.

"I'm sorry, Moms. I had to give them our food. The frog hunter said he'd make Reddy bleed if I didn't. First Reddy, then Dan. That's what he said."

"Oh, my poor Bobby," Mrs. Belden mourned.

"I have to get back to conduct a search at the inn," the sergeant said wearily. "There were two robberies there tonight."

"Miss Ryks?" Trixie asked.

"How did you know? Somebody took all that junk she wears. Their real haul was Mrs. Boyer's diamond jewelry."

"Th-That isn't what I meant," Trixie stammered, then thought to herself, *I was sure Miss Ryks was the thief.*

"Hallie," Trixie whispered as she faced her cousin,

"this thing is too big for us. We need some help. With police all over the inn, Miss Ryks'll have to stay in that wheelchair. She can't do anything to Dan tonight."

"What are you talking about?" Brian demanded, hollow-eyed from lack of sleep, tonight's alarm, and the long strain of the search for Dan Mangan.

"Yesterday, Hallie, Honey, and I found the missing comic that the sergeant suspects of directing a gang of thieves," Trixie announced, and she turned to Sergeant Molinson. "You're right. He does—plus he's Miss Ryks."

The sergeant looked skeptical.

"Listen to me, please!" Trixie begged.

When the story had been told, from the wheelchair on Glen Road to the gang in the shed, Molinson rubbed his forehead. "All I can say is that I'll keep a man on duty outside the door of room two-fourteen—"

"—outside the windows, too!" Trixie interrupted. "That's how she kept in touch with the gang, when she wasn't playing the role of Dick Ryks and scaring little boys out of their wits out here in our woods!"

"The windows, too," the sergeant conceded. "Since I'll be a guest at the wedding tomorrow, I'll be on hand in case something goes wrong. Mr. Wheeler's asked for a guard for the gift display. I suppose I can spare two men. They won't be needed at room two-fourteen anyway, if Miss Ryks is at the wedding. Well, I have a long night ahead of me. I'll see you all at the wedding tomorrow."

When the kitchen door closed, Trixie said resentfully, "He doesn't believe me."

Mr. Belden tried to reason with her. "You have to admit that the idea of an invalid in a wheelchair tramping through the woods organizing robberies is pretty farfetched."

"Dad!" Trixie wailed. "We saw her with our own eyes! She changed from a woman to a man just by changing wigs and taking off that long dress!"

"And now you've been threatened," Mrs. Belden said slowly. "Oh, Peter! Maybe we shouldn't go to the wedding tomorrow."

"We're all in the ceremony," Brian quietly said to his mother. "We have to go."

"Do be careful, all of you," Mrs. Belden begged.

A night of restless sleep stretched ahead of Trixie. She asked Hallie to sleep in the extra bed in her room.

Hallie's berry-black eyes glistened. "Trixie, you've never asked me that before."

"So now I'm asking," Trixie said.

Several times during the night, Trixie awoke from a nightmare about a room filled with watching eyes. Once she called out, "Bobby!"

She was comforted by Hallie's answer: "Bobby's safe. Go back to sleep." When morning came, Hallie was still there.

Trixie apologized. "Did I keep you awake?"

"I love Bobby, too," Hallie reminded her. "He's my cousin. That matters."

"Yes." Trixie thought of all the quarrels she'd had

with Hallie. They weren't important any longer. Both of them were growing up. Each was becoming her own person—one blond and pert, the other darkly beautiful; one with a firecracker temper, the other matter-of-fact. But both loved people, and both were loyal to family and friends. Trixie couldn't find the words to tell Hallie what she was thinking. She could only smile at her cousin and watch those incredibly dark eyes begin to glow.

Almost shyly, Hallie asked, "Do you ever wonder who you are?"

"Yes. You, too?" Trixie asked softly.

"Do you sometimes feel like you're standing all alone on a mountaintop with a cold wind blowing? You shout into the wind, but your words get pushed back down your throat. You know you'll keep swallowing your own words till you can answer the question, 'Who am I?' But there's no one to tell you the answer."

Hallie sounded so lost and lonely that Trixie's eyes misted. "I don't know much about mountaintops," she said. "I have the feeling that I'm in a glass box. All of the people in the world march past me, but I can't join them because of the glass. I know that when I can tell just one person who I am, the glass will melt and I can join the parade. It's hard being a teen-ager, isn't it?"

"I'll bet you want to be a detective because you want to keep the parade marching safely," Hallie guessed.

"Do you think so? Brian and Mart say it's because I'm so nosy."

"My mom would call you a truth seeker," Hallie said. "My mom has the smarts, so I go along with her most of the time. At home, Cap and Knut treat me like one of the fellows. I was getting so mixed-up, Mom said I needed some close contact with another girl. I thought of you, Trixie, so that's why I came."

"Really?" Trixie gulped. "I'm sorry I was rough on you."

"If you think you're rough, you should try living with Cap Belden," Hallie retorted. "Come on. Let's get up. Breakfast smells good."

At the breakfast table, Mr. Belden tapped the newspaper. "The Teed people are cleared of any guilt in the matter of transporting stolen goods. They simply took an order over the phone."

Trixie slid into her chair and picked up her napkin. "I never did think that driver was a thief. He talks too much. He couldn't keep a secret if he tried." She heaved a sigh up from her very toes. "I thought Juliana's wedding day would be the happiest day of the whole summer. Now look at it! That gang and their boss are out there somewhere, and Dan's missing."

"Yes, look at it!" Mrs. Belden lilted. "Bobby's safe. You're safe. The weather's perfect. There's not a cloud in the sky. It won't rain on all those beautiful dresses and flowers and—"

"And guests?" Brian prompted. He glanced up at the clock. "Hey, Hallie, see what time it is! We have to pick up the Bob-Whites' gift at the jewelers in an hour."

The Bob-Whites had chosen to give Juliana and Hans a silver music box engraved with all their names. Its cost had drained the treasury, but nobody minded.

"It's a long time till the wedding," Hallie told Brian. "A lot can happen before four-thirty."

" 'Friday, the sixth of August, at half after four o'clock,' " Mark intoned in a poetry-reading voice.

" 'Quoth the Raven, "Nevermore," ' " Hallie quoted impishly.

Trixie frowned. "Don't say that, Hallie. I never did like that raven."

"Honey called," Mrs. Belden told Trixie. "She's expecting all of you early."

"No problem, Auntie," Hallie said. "We're all taken care of. Baths, hair, fingernails, toenails—the works."

"Hallie, you wouldn't dare wear that green stuff on your toenails to a wedding!" Trixie shouted.

"Want to bet?" Hallie drawled and left the kitchen on the run.

Trixie leaped up to wrestle Hallie to a couch, shouting, "Bobby, help me! Untie Hallie's sneaker and see if her toes are green!"

In the noisy scramble that followed, Bobby removed Hallie's shoe. "Huh! They're just like everybody else's toes," he grumbled.

"What's the matter with that?" Brian teased.

"I wanted 'em to be green, like usual," Bobby said.

The romp dispelled some of Trixie's uneasiness. Ordinarily, she would have told Honey all the details about last night's ordeal, but when she reached Manor House, she couldn't bear to spoil one minute of her best friend's happy day. She followed Honey to the sewing room to help Ella down the stairs.

They found Ella Kline on the floor, her crutches beyond her reach. Both girls ran to her rescue. "I skidded," she said as she dizzily sat up. "Hand me my crutches, please?"

"You need your wheelchair!" Trixie stormed, thinking of the way Miss Ryks had strode around that bedroom, puffing on a cigar.

"Yes," Ella agreed. "I've needed it for a long time, but I couldn't afford it till I got the job at the Bride's Shop. Right this minute, I need new crutch tips. I have some in my room at the inn. They're in a dresser drawer."

Honey held out her hand when Ella was safely seated in the rocking chair. "If you want to give me the key to your room, I'll see that someone goes after them during the first break we have."

"The manager will have to let you in," Ella said. "I haven't seen my key since Dick Ryks gave me a check for the wheelchair and I asked him to put it in my purse, which was out of my reach. Sometimes I have to depend on others. That's just the way it is."

"You'll have your wheelchair very soon," Trixie promised. "Miss Ryks is leaving the inn this week."

"Honey! Trixie!" Miss Trask appeared in the doorway, waving the notebook she had carried from the day Juliana had chosen her wedding date. "Di's waiting for us downstairs. We have work to do."

For the rest of the morning, Trixie worked indoors. She found herself inventing reasons to go near a window. Uneasily, she studied the smoothly mowed lawns, the freshly clipped shrubbery, and the parking lot Tom had arranged between the stable and the house. If even one member of that gang slipped onto the Manor House grounds without detection, there'd be trouble. She listened for sounds that were out of the ordinary. She studied the names and handwriting on the packages she laid on the long gift table in the alcove where the Bob-Whites had gathered the night of the Lynch robbery.

"You're as skittery as a cat," Jim told her as he placed a large bowl of daisies on the table. "Something's wrong."

Trixie opened her mouth to deny the charge, then sighed instead. She knew that Jim could read her face and manner like the pages of a primer. With a quick glance to be sure they were alone, she told him of Bobby's ordeal and of the escape of the gang. "And there's still Ella's wheelchair and that two-headed fraud, Miss Ryks!"

Jim didn't scowl at her burst of venom. "Honey told me about the masquerade. She suspects, and I agree with her, that Miss Ryks stole Mrs. Boyer's diamonds and ditched her own paste jewelry to draw suspicion away from herself."

Trixie nodded. "It has to be like that. I wish I knew

why she's coming to the wedding."

"So do I," Jim said. "I'll feel better when the police get here to take charge of this room. There's enough stuff here for a bang-up yard sale!"

Trixie widened her round blue eyes. "I'll bet that's it, Jim! That Oliver Tolliver steals wedding invitations when he can so that he'll have entry to the houses where the gifts are on display."

"And the gifts are unwrapped, so he can tell which are really valuable," Jim agreed. "Well! Maybe we've foiled him this time. Here come Molinson's men."

For a few minutes, Trixie almost felt safe. The policemen were in plain clothes, but they looked as if they knew how to handle an emergency.

Lunch was Juliana's last meal as Miss Maasden. Of the Bob-Whites, only Dan Mangan was absent, and Bobby took his place at the table. After the previous night's fright, the youngest Belden was unusually quiet.

After lunch, the Bob-Whites worked in the garden. The minute that shade slanted across the bower, they placed a dozen baskets of daisies, golden-centered and wax-petaled, around it. The altar Regan had built was spread with the same white linen cloth that had been used at the Wheelers' own wedding. Mrs. Vanderpoel supplied the top cloth of handmade lace. For sentiment's sake, Mrs. Belden lent her best candlesticks.

At three o'clock, Miss Trask declared everything in readiness. "It's time to dress. I thank each and every one of you for your help. Now, let's enjoy the wedding, shall we?"

I'll try, Trixie thought.

Slowly, she walked through the garden and took a long look at the wonderland that had been created there. Between the altar in the bower and the bridal table on the terrace by the birdbath, rows of folding chairs waited for guests. Drifting butterflies, shadows of bird wings, and bursts of song made the scene so beautiful that Trixie felt like crying.

She headed toward the house. As she passed the organ that had been set by the terrace entrance, she thought, *At four-thirty, I'll walk down that aisle of flowers. But what will Miss Ryks be doing?* Trixie shivered.

She met Sergeant Molinson in the lower hall of the house. He looked tired but alert. "About last night, Trixie—don't you think you let that imagination of yours run away with you? We searched Miss Ryks's room. There was no makeup or men's clothing there."

Uh-oh! Trixie thought. *She did see us in that mirror.*

"Her jewelry isn't as valuable as Mrs. Boyer's, but it's still missing. Now, I've had a call from her nephew asking me to please pick up his aunt because she doesn't want to miss the wedding of old friends. If she were a fraud, why would she deliberately put herself in such close contact with the police?"

Trixie didn't argue. Plainly, Sergeant Molinson didn't buy her theory. *So it's up to me to prove Miss Ryks guilty,* Trixie decided. *But how? If Miss Ryks escapes today, there'll be other country club acts, other robberies, and other little boys like Bobby in danger. Other teen-agers will be recruited from the streets and trained in crime. She'll go on and on, becoming more skilled and causing more trouble.*

Trixie brought herself up short when she realized that she was thinking "she," even though she knew Miss Ryks was the comic, Oliver Tolliver. He or she—did it matter which pronoun was used? This actor was playing out his role till the final curtain dropped.

Trixie ran to the door to call to the sergeant before he left the porte cochere. "When you go to get Miss Ryks, will you please pick up Ella Kline's crutch tips? They're in her room at the inn."

"No need," the sergeant called back. "Hallie went after them."

"Did someone take her?"

As he drove away, the sergeant shouted, "I understand that she rode a bicycle."

Hallie!

Riding to the Glen Road Inn while Miss Ryks was still in residence was like running headlong into a hornet's nest. Oh! That was just like a—a Belden! Hallie certainly knew better than to go alone after having promised Brian and Mart to honor the buddy system. But knowing better would not keep her safe.

Suddenly Trixie realized that Hallie's safety was just as important to her as Bobby's. Hallie was family.

What can I do? Trixie worried. *What can I do?*

A Wedding and a Wheelchair · 14

DI AND HONEY rushed down the hall and swept Trixie along with them up the stairs and into the sewing room, where they were to dress.

As she'd been doing all day, Trixie hurried to the window as soon as she could. Down on the lawn, she could see Brian, Mart, Bobby, and Jim with Hans. They were standing straight to protect the perfect creases in their formal outfits. She saw them wave to her father, who was to take Dan's place. Matt Wheeler's red hair shone when he crossed a patch of sunlight to join the group. Their work done for the day, Regan, Mr. Maypenny, and Tom walked up from the stable, wearing their best clothes. The men in Trixie's life were safe. That is, all but Dan. . . .

Trixie tried to push worry aside and enjoy the moment, as Miss Trask had advised. Just the same, the minute she was dressed, she went back to the window.

Honey joined her there and said, "They are beautiful, aren't they?" Then she hugged Trixie and added, "So are we!"

Trixie had to agree. Her friends seemed to float in their tissue-thin cotton dresses, their sashes and hat streamers providing the color that was perfect for each girl. Di was used to being told she was pretty, and so was Honey, but even they looked at each other with extra appreciation.

"Guests are beginning to arrive. Let's all go see Juliana one more time," Honey decided.

In a happy rush of fluttering ribbons, Trixie, Di, and Honey ran to Juliana's room. Mrs. Vanderpoel had come early to help the bride dress. Mrs. Wheeler and Mrs. Lynch were there to provide a borrowed lace handkerchief and a blue satin garter.

With a lump in her throat, Trixie stopped in the doorway. Out of an earlier time when life was simpler came this happy bride. Healthy skin glowed through strips of handmade lace in throatband and sleeves. The skirt was pulled into long soft pleats by bands of heavy lace, made while a girl waited for a war to end. A wisp of gauzelike veiling seemed to float over the daisy-wreathed white hat. Tiny, dainty, and demure, Juliana Maasden had never looked lovelier.

Mrs. Vanderpoel clasped one of Juliana's hands. "If

I had a daughter, I'd want her to look just like you, Juliana."

"Thank you, Mrs. Vanderpoel," Juliana whispered. "Thank you all for our beautiful, beautiful wedding."

Miss Trask hurried into the room. "Where's Hallie Belden?" she cried. "It's almost time for the march to start. I've been presenting the guest book, but I can't do everything!"

"A-Ask Moms to take charge," Trixie stammered.

Tom had come upstairs to help Ella Kline, and Trixie followed them down the stairs. He carried Ella in his arms as she held her crutches. When they reached the terrace, Tom gently put her down, and Mart carefully accompanied her to a chair with arms. He stood the crutches upright against the side of the chair. Once more, Trixie was stabbed with resentment against someone who would take advantage of a helpless person.

For over an hour, the organist had provided a concert of familiar love songs. Near the organ, Celia had charge of the children in the wedding procession. Di's small sisters fidgeted with the daisy wreaths in their long hair, and Bobby guarded his satin ring pillow with his life. Trixie heard him tell the tiny girls, "The ring's tied on this pillow so those robber kids can't take it. They took Di's radio, but I won't let them take the ring." Each child regarded Bobby with wide-eyed respect, knowing what it felt like to be robbed.

When Trixie took her place in the line forming in

the lower hall, Jim stopped beside her. He said in a low voice, "I've just checked the gift display. Everything's okay." He took a step, then turned back to say, "You look as pretty as Juliana." Trixie blushed with pleasure.

Together they watched Sergeant Molinson walk beside Miss Ryks's wheelchair as Brian pushed it all the way to the center of the audience. Miss Ryks looked regal in a dove gray costume with a chin-high collar, long sleeves, and a long, full skirt. She wore her customary dark glasses.

When Trixie exhaled a worried breath, Jim asked, "What are we going to do?"

"I don't know," Trixie said soberly. "Keep our eyes open and be ready, I guess."

"I'm with you," Jim promised, then hurried to the summerhouse to join the pastor and Hans.

Trixie watched Mart seat the family of the president of her father's bank. Brian escorted Juliana's friends, the De Jongs, who had cut short their vacation in the Poconos. Now it was time to seat Mrs. Wheeler, who was substituting as mother of the bride.

Suddenly the wedding march began, startling the birds into a burst of song. It was Friday, the sixth of August, at half after four o'clock.

Trixie wasn't prepared for the adult looks on her brothers' faces when they led the march down the curving path of flat stones. They were followed by Di and Honey, who hooked fingers before leaving the hall. Juliana had wanted a simple procession, so each person walked along the path at his or her own pace.

Trixie began to move forward. She kept her eyes on the pastor, who stood behind the altar and held the Wheelers' own white Bible. Tall and blond, Hans waited in the bower of daisies for Juliana. Beside him stood Jim, with sun slanting on his red hair.

At Trixie's heels danced the Lynch twins, scattering flower petals. They giggled, but Bobby marched solemnly, much aware of his responsibility.

When she passed the table where her mother presided over the guest book, Trixie's brain beat a wild tattoo. *Where's Hallie? Where's Hallie?*

Trixie reached the altar and waited for Mr. Wheeler to come down the path with Juliana.

On the walk down the aisle of flowers, Matthew Wheeler paused to break a blossom from a plant. He waved it in front of Juliana's face, trying to make the rather nervous bride smile. Trixie heard Juliana's little giggle of surprise. All heads turned toward the bride, and every face beamed with delight.

Trixie smiled, but just for a moment. Her ears had caught the muffled hum of a motor, not in the parking lot where it might indicate a latecomer, but someplace out of sight near the bicycle rack. She found herself standing on tiptoe, straining for a glimpse of something happening on the opposite side of the house. Jim noticed her tension. His face went blank while he, too, listened.

When Mr. Wheeler had performed his duty as "father of the bride," he sat beside his wife and gave her the fragrant blossom he had picked.

The ceremony was simple and profoundly moving. Trixie was sure she would remember the vows forever. Yet when the pastor said, "May I present Mr. and Mrs. Hans Vorwald," every word was erased from her mind.

Right before the Bob-Whites' eyes, Juliana had changed in such important ways. She had come into the valley as Janie, the girl with no memory. Next, she was Juliana Maasden, Jim's only living relative. Now she was Mrs. Hans Vorwald, whose home was in Amsterdam.

The loud and joyous recessional music started, and Juliana and Hans walked slowly down the path. Holding hands, they smiled at each other and at friends.

Trixie and Jim each took six steps and met at the altar. When she put her gloved hand on Jim's jacket sleeve, Trixie felt the trembling of his arm. Jim, too, had been deeply moved by the ceremony.

"So beautiful," Trixie murmured. Jim nodded.

As they faced the guests and began to walk back down the path, Jim asked, "The receiving line will take several minutes, won't it?"

"Of course," Trixie said. "All the guests will go through it."

"I have to check the bags and be sure Tom has the car ready to take Hans and Juliana to the airport. Then there's something I have to investigate. I'll get Mart and Brian to help me."

"You heard the sound of a motor?" Trixie didn't try

197

to be more specific. She wasn't sure exactly what she'd heard when the organ had played its loudest.

Again Jim nodded. "I couldn't keep my eyes off Miss Ryks. For some reason, she's demanding all of Sergeant Molinson's attention."

"I'll keep track of her while you're gone," Trixie said. Even as they talked, both Trixie and Jim nodded and smiled at guests.

When they reached the lower hall, Trixie ran back outdoors to the small table where her mother sat. "Moms, has anybody seen Hallie? Did she come back from the inn?"

"No," Mrs. Belden answered soberly. "I can't imagine what happened to her. Miss Trask called the inn. The clerk said Hallie stopped at the desk for Ella's key, but she didn't return it." When Trixie gasped her dismay, her mother's voice took on a reassuring tone. "Enjoy the reception, dear. The adults are taking care of this problem now. Matthew sent one of the policemen who was guarding the gifts to find Hallie and bring her back. You know Hallie. She probably took the woods path home and is spending all this time pushing her bicycle uphill the whole way."

"Moms!" Trixie moaned. "Hallie may be in danger! She keeps promises. She'd be here to take charge of the guest book if she could. Oh! First Dan, and now Hallie!"

"What can happen?" Mrs. Belden asked. "Miss Ryks is sitting right there with Sergeant Molinson. There are also police at the inn investigating the robbery."

"There's that gang!" Trixie said shakily.

"Without their boss, what can they do?" asked her mother reasonably. "If, indeed, Miss Ryks is their boss. Look at her. Doesn't it seem improbable?"

Trixie's heart sank. Even her mother doubted her theory. She protested, "But I saw—"

"Hurry!" said Mrs. Belden. "The receiving line is forming."

Trixie stood between Juliana and Honey in the line. Worried though she was, her breath caught each time she heard Hans say, "This is my wife, Juliana." Once he said indulgently, "This is like greeting guests on an ordinary Sunday afternoon."

Juliana giggled. "Not in Amsterdam, I promise you. I won't know two hundred people for years!"

Honey whispered, "Something's bothering you, Trixie Belden. I can tell."

"Oh, Honey!" Trixie whispered back. "If only you knew!" She stood on tiptoe, trying to see what her brothers were doing. Had they gone with Jim? No. They were circulating among the guests, performing their duties as ushers. And Miss Ryks? Where was she? Oh. There she was. The sergeant was pushing the old fraud's chair.

When Miss Ryks came through the receiving line, Hans raised her hand to brush it with his lips, and Juliana kissed her forehead. As soon as the elderly woman was beyond earshot, Juliana said, "Hans, we never did find out whose family she knew!"

In the folds of her white dress, Trixie crossed her fingers. *I hope,* she prayed desperately, *I can keep her from spoiling the wedding.* When Trixie saw a flash of pink, her hopes rose for a moment, but it wasn't Hallie's ribbon sash. Mrs. DeJong was wearing pink accessories.

After all the photographs had been taken, at least thirty young people followed Juliana into the lower hall. Lightly she ran up the stairs and paused, holding her bouquet high. Hans stood by the newel-post, watching her. Juliana buried her face in her bouquet for a last fragrant sniff, blew a kiss to Hans, then threw her flowers. Many hands reached for it, but it was Di who captured the bridal bouquet.

"Next to be married!" someone sang out, and Di giggled.

Trixie stayed with Honey and Di long enough to touch and smell the flowers, then hurried back to the lawn to keep her promise to Jim.

She saw him beckon Mart and Brian, and the three of them disappeared through the swinging doors that led to the part of the house where the wedding gifts were displayed.

With the ring safely on Juliana's finger, Bobby was relieved of his responsibility. He left the flower girls and followed Trixie to Miss Ryks's chair. There he stood slightly to the right and scowled at the person in the chair.

Trixie made the usual "Wasn't it lovely?" comment to Miss Ryks and the sergeant and turned to Bobby.

He was openly staring, and one never knew what he might say. Trixie reminded Miss Ryks that she had met Bobby at the shower. Miss Ryks didn't bother to wheeze an answer but only nodded regally.

Suddenly Bobby said, "She looks like somebody I know."

Miss Ryks's whole body stiffened, and Trixie wished she could see through those dark glasses. The elderly woman laid a big hand on the sergeant's sleeve. Looking at an ancient watch on a chain, she said breathily, "Thank you, Sergeant Molinson, for your help. My nephew's sending a taxi to pick me up. If you'll please go to the parking lot and tell the driver where to find me, I'll meet him at the porte cochere."

Quickly, Trixie estimated distances. The porte cochere was out of sight of the wedding guests. A trip to the parking lot would put the sergeant beyond contact for a few minutes. Whatever this—this *person* was planning must be going according to some previously arranged schedule.

"You must stay for the refreshments," Trixie said hastily. "You'll want to see Juliana cut the cake."

Miss Ryks ignored Trixie. "If you please, Sergeant?"

Obediently the sergeant left his folding chair and strode off down a path that would lead him to the parking lot. Trixie felt a moment of panic, knowing he would never have gone had he not believed Miss Ryks to be a helpless cripple. *I have to hand it to you,* Trixie thought. *You're a pretty good actor to be able to fool the sergeant.* Aloud she said, "Miss Ryks, you

201

really must have a cup of punch before you go."

Miss Ryks fanned her thickly made-up face. "It *is* hot," she agreed. "Please push me."

Even with Bobby's help, pushing Miss Ryks was no easy task. When they reached the terrace, where the picnic table had been transformed into a bridal table, both Trixie and Bobby heaved sighs of relief, and Trixie paused to straighten her hat and gloves.

Hans and Juliana took their places behind the towering wedding cake, and the guests surged forward to watch the silver knife cut the first slice. Juliana stood on tiptoe to feed Hans his first bite of food as a married man. Cameras flashed, people laughed, and hands pattered happy applause.

Miss Ryks gripped the arms of the wheelchair as if to rise, then settled back as stiff as a broom handle. She said coldly, "My dear Trixie, I simply must reach the porte cochere to meet that taxi."

"Just a minute, Miss Ryks. The newlyweds will have their punch, and then I can bring you a cup."

Miss Ryks opened the large purse that lay in her lap. Standing at her shoulder, Trixie was just tall enough to look down into it. Sunlight glinted on a shining mass that Miss Ryks quickly covered with a handkerchief. As the handkerchief was moved, Trixie could see an open moneybag. That bag held something, just as Bobby had said, but that something wasn't a frog dying for want of air—it was a small gun.

Trixie's pulse pounded in her throat. What had Jim said about guns like this? "Trigger can be set to go off if you blow on it." *So don't blow!* she warned herself sternly.

"Bobby?" Trixie tried to keep her voice from trembling. "Will you please go find Jim? I think he went to speak to someone at the gift table."

There was no mistaking Miss Ryks's reaction to Trixie's words. She kept her purse open with her hand close to the gun in the moneybag. When Bobby was out of immediate danger, Trixie began pushing the wheelchair very slowly toward the table where the punch bowl sat in a bank of daisies. Instead of avoiding people, Trixie crowded the bulky chair into groups. She spoke to friends and neighbors, introducing Miss Ryks and calling attention to her presence. Miss Ryks could only sit stiffly, nod, wheeze, and mutter, "Trixie Belden! I told you that I'm ready to leave. At once!"

Trixie cooed politely while keeping her eye on the door. Would Jim never come back?

At long last Jim came running out. Mart and Brian were right behind him.

"Trixie!" Jim burst out. Trixie put her fingers to her lips and pointed at Miss Ryks's back. Jim forced himself to whisper. "The wedding gifts are gone, and so are the guards!"

Trixie wasn't surprised. She'd known something would happen. "One guard went to find Hallie," she whispered back. "I think Miss Ryks is trying to get away to meet the gang. What shall we do?"

"Stop her!" Jim hissed.

Trixie knew that Miss Ryks must have heard something of the whispered conversation because she started to turn around. Hastily Trixie said, "Sit still, Miss Ryks. Jim will help me take you to the porte cochere."

Jim took the hint and helped push the chair out of sight of the wedding festivity. Mart and Brian walked behind the chair, obeying Trixie's beckoning hands.

Sergeant Molinson was in the taxi that entered the porte cochere. He left the cab to help Miss Ryks to her feet.

Jim acted instantly. He slammed against the side of the wheelchair with all his healthy young weight. Already half standing, Miss Ryks was thrown off-balance. Out went her hands, the one for balance, the other to rescue her dark glasses. Trixie snatched the big purse, moneybag and all, and handed it to Mart. "Run!" she ordered, and Mart ran.

Cornered, Miss Ryks discarded her role as cripple and jumped up to plunge after Mart. Trixie and Jim acted as with one mind. Just as Miss Ryks leaped forward, both planted their feet on the long gray skirt.

Rrrrr-rip!

A man's rolled-up trousers were suddenly exposed above large white oxfords. Miss Ryks threw a punch at Jim, but he ducked. Brian closed in from the rear, and together the two boys struggled with the angry guest.

Miss Ryks broke free and tried to run. Using the wheelchair as a surprise weapon, Trixie pushed it as fast as she could into the path of the escaping gang leader. Hampered by the trailing skirt and tripped up by the wheelchair, the former invalid was overcome when Sergeant Molinson helped the struggling boys.

Trixie did the one thing that she had wanted to do from the minute she saw Miss Ryks's two-headed act in room 214—she snatched the blue white wig from Miss Ryks's head. As Trixie had suspected, that action revealed not the brassy hair of the nephew, Dick Ryks. It revealed the bald head of the man who had pushed the wheelchair down Glen Road and bought the rope at the sporting goods store!

Finding himself totally unmasked, the comic from the country club took off the tight high collar, and Miss Ryks, room 214, Glen Road Inn, disappeared forever.

The sergeant rubbed his forehead. "I don't believe it, Detective Belden! This character had me fooled."

"I'll take that as a compliment to my acting ability," the actor snarled.

"You are good, you know," Trixie said. "It's just too bad you didn't stay on the stage where you belong."

Bobby had seen the quick exit of the wheelchair parade and now appeared at the porte cochere. Soberly he stared at the captured man. "I knew he wasn't a frog hunter," Bobby said. "Frogs can't breathe in a moneybag."

"But guns can," Trixie told Sergeant Molinson. "Mart doesn't know it, but he's also carrying around Mrs. Boyer's diamonds."

"Which I am more than glad to relinquish," Mart declared, handing the large purse to the sergeant.

When Jim explained about the stolen wedding gifts, Sergeant Molinson called Regan.

"Pretty smart," the policeman told the actor, "keeping me busy while your gang worked."

"Miss Ryks" smirked.

When Regan arrived, he said, "There's a truck parked down by the clubhouse. Obviously the gang's waiting for the boss. I'll call Tom and have him head them off by turning a car across the road. Up here, we'll use this taxi. Simple."

Taken by surprise, Dan's old street gang was captured with little difficulty. The truck was driven back to the French doors of the alcove, and willing hands replaced the wedding gifts on the display tables. The missing guard was found bound and gagged in a closet.

Few wedding guests knew of the action in the porte cochere, and by the time family groups began drifting back to their cars, Tom was on hand to help with smiling courtesy. A short while later, he drove Mr. and Mrs. Hans Vorwald, on their way to a new life in Amsterdam, away from Manor House and onto Glen Road.

"Good-bye! Good luck!" The Bob-Whites shouted and waved, unabashed by the tears dampening their cheeks.

"Thank you! Bless you!" Hans and Juliana called back to them.

Trixie turned at once to clutch Honey's arm. "We have to find Hallie and Dan! The gang members aren't going to tell where they hid them. They'll want to bargain with that information for their own advantage! We can be sure of that!"

"Are we sure Miss Ryks hid them?" Di asked.

Trixie nodded. "Miss Ryks, the wheelchair, the robberies—there's no way to talk about one without the others, so I'm sure! Oliver Tolliver needed a quick way to disappear from the country club after Dan found that note in the fireplace. When he caught a ride with the Teed driver, he must have meant only to hide the wheelchair and collect a reward, but then he saw the chance to rent the chair from Ella Kline and turn himself into a sick old woman—a clever disguise. To keep in touch with the gang, though, he had to be two people. He couldn't move around freely in a wheelchair."

"And he pulled the scrawny kid through the window whenever he needed a messenger," Honey reminded her.

"Right," Trixie agreed. "He reported a burglary attempt, then made sure that the police suspected Dan."

Brian interrupted. "That should prove Dan isn't working with the gang. They wouldn't make a scapegoat of one of their own members."

"That's right," Jim said. "Dan must have caught them in the game preserve, and they had to find some way to keep him quiet."

Mart spoke so earnestly that, for once, he forgot to

use long words. "We know how the gang lived. Bobby fed them. And we know their contact was Dick Ryks. What else do we know about that nephew character? He didn't get around much in Sleepyside."

"Well," Honey said slowly, "Ella Kline lives at the inn, and her key disappeared when Dick Ryks put a check in her purse."

"That's it!" Trixie shrieked. "The desk clerk said Dick Ryks was visiting someone *up on the third floor!* That's where Hallie and Dan must be—locked in Ella Kline's room! The police didn't go there while investigating the diamond robbery because they knew Ella was here at Manor House!"

"Let's go!" Jim shouted.

Within minutes, Jim, Brian, Mart, Di, Honey, and Trixie, still dressed in wedding finery, clustered around the desk clerk at Glen Road Inn. "We need to get into Ella Kline's room," Trixie demanded. When the man started to protest, Trixie shouted, "It's a matter of life and death! Hurry!"

The clerk gave in, fished out a key, and led the way to the third floor. He muttered the whole time about whether it was ethical to open an absent guest's door. "Twice in one day! I could get fired."

When the door to Ella's room swung open, two pairs of dark eyes stared out, first showing apprehension, then joy.

"Hallie!" Trixie cried. She ran to a rocking chair where her cousin sat, a gag in her mouth and her hands tied behind her back.

Jim, Brian, and Mart rushed to cut the ropes that spread-eagled Dan flat on his back on the bed. He, too, was gagged, as well as groggy and weak from lack of exercise and not enough food.

"Your poor, poor wrists," Trixie moaned when she set Hallie free.

"You should see Dan's!" doctor-to-be Brian said angrily.

The incredulous desk clerk watched the scene from the doorway.

"Oh, Dan!" Trixie cried. "We've hunted, and worried, and thought, and hunted again!"

As he sat up and dangled his long legs over the edge of the bed, Dan said weakly, "Thanks. H-Have you g-got something for a dry mouth?" He tried to smile. Silently Honey brought a glass of water from the bathroom, and Di held it while Dan sipped. After a while, he was able to say, "I'm fine. They untied me once or twice a day."

"Why didn't you make a break for it?" Mart asked.

"Would you have wanted Bobby tied up here in my place?" Dan asked. "That's what they threatened, and I couldn't stand to have that happen."

"Hallie, how did *you* get caught?" Di asked.

Hallie turned from Ella's dresser. "My mom has the smarts, but she didn't tell me that empty hotel rooms aren't always empty! The minute I unlocked that door, the scrawny kid—can you believe it?—that little runt grabbed me, stuck a gag in my mouth, and tied me to the rocking chair." Hallie stood her tallest to express her amazement that such a thing could have happened to her.

"He heard you coming, Hallie," Dan said comfortingly. "I couldn't warn you. I tried, but he made sure that my gag was tight."

"See?" Hallie told the sober Bob-Whites. "I told you Dan's an okay kid."

"And so are you, Hallie Belden," Honey said warmly.

Brian and Jim helped Dan down the stairs, and Mart walked with Hallie, in case her knees got wobbly. "My feet went to sleep," she explained. She patted the pocket of her shorts. "Anyway, I got what I came for—Ella's crutch tips."

"She has a wheelchair now," Di told her happily.

When they reached the desk, Trixie said, "Please, may I make a telephone call? And we do want to thank you for helping us."

"Little lady, I had no idea—" The clerk rubbed his head, picked up his crossword puzzle book, and put it down again. "Well, I just had no idea what was going on."

"Plenty!" Trixie said briskly. "You'll read all about it in the *Sleepyside Sun!*"

Having been notified that Dan was safe, Regan and Mr. Maypenny couldn't wait to see him, and they met the Bob-White station wagon on Glen Road, near the Lynch mailbox.

Both Regan and Mr. Maypenny jumped from the Wheeler car, followed by Matthew Wheeler and Peter and Bobby Belden. All the Bob-Whites exploded from the station wagon.

Peter Belden hurried to touch his niece's thin face to make sure she was no mirage. Bobby wavered between Dan and Hallie, then went to investigate the mailbox. "There's no mail today," he announced.

Weak though he was, Dan met his uncle and the old gamekeeper in the middle of the road, glad to feel the comfort and strength in their hands and arms. He looked at the flower in Mr. Maypenny's buttonhole and asked wistfully, "The wedding's over? Did Juliana get her ring back?"

He turned to Regan. "I'm sorry, Uncle Bill! I had to take the ring to keep those creeps from stealing it. The boss has a thing about diamonds. That night at the farm, Reddy let me know that he was somewhere near. When I had the chance to take the ring, I slid it off Juliana's finger. I couldn't stand to see her cry, but I couldn't let anybody know what was going on till I tried to round up that gang and keep them from ruining the wedding.

"I planned to hide the ring and a note in Jim's saddlebag, but Tom needed help with Jupiter just then, and I stuffed the ring in your desk. I was on my way back to get it when I saw one of the gang hanging around. I took off after him and chased him all the way to the inn. He got into the building through a window. I figured out that he was in room two-fourteen and watched it from the hallway inside. When that Dick Ryks came out, I followed him up to the third floor. He jumped me, and—you know how that turned out. I've learned that I'd better stick to working on the game preserve. I'm not very good as a detective!"

"Leave that job to the Belden-Wheeler Detective Agency!" Jim advised proudly.

"Don't forget the Bob-Whites and Hallie," Honey chimed in.

Hallie's berry-black eyes warmed with affection. "You're a bunch of okay kids. You've got the smarts!"

"No, Hallie, that's not quite right." Trixie did her best imitation of a drawl and linked arms with her new friend. "You're an okay kid yourself!"

"Oh, jeeps," Hallie chuckled.

"That's *gleeps!*" the Bob-Whites chorused.